AUNT JANE'S NIECES ABROAD

By
L. FRANK BAUM
(AKA EDITH VAN DYNE)

Aunt Jane's Nieces Abroad

by **L. Frank Baum (AKA Edith Van Dyne)**

Copyright © 2023

All Rights reserved.
No part of this publication may be reproduced, stored in a retrieval system, or transmitted in any form or by any means, electronic, mechanical, photocopying or Otherwise, without the written permission of the publisher.

The author/editor asserts the moral right to be identified as the author/editor of this work.

ISBN: 978-93-57279-15-4

Published by

DOUBLE 9 BOOKS

2/13-B, Ansari Road, Daryaganj
New Delhi – 110002
info@double9books.com
www.double9books.com
Tel. 011-40042856

This book is under public domain

ABOUT THE AUTHOR

Lyman Frank Baum was an American writer best known for his children's books, especially The Wonderful Wizard of Oz and its sequels. He wrote 14 novels in the Oz series, plus 41 other novels, 83 short stories, above 200 poems, and at least 42 scripts. He made many attempts to lead his works to the stage and screen; the 1939 adaptation of the first Oz book became a milestone of 20th-century cinema. Baum was born on 15 May 1856, near Syracuse, New York. His father, Benjamin, was a rich oil businessman, and young Frank developed in comfort. As a young child Frank was teached at home with his kins, but at the age of 12 he was sent to study at Peekskill Military Academy. He followed a variety of careers varying from acting to newspaper reporting to theatrical management to writing plays. Baum married Maud Gage, daughter of Matilda Joslyn Gage, a famous women's suffrage campaigner. His famous works are Mother Goose, Father Goose, The Wonderful Wizard of Oz, The Life and Adventures of Santa Claus, The Master Key, etc. He made and headed The Oz Film Manufacturing Company in 1914. Baum expired on 6 May 1919 and was buried in Glendale, California.

CONTENTS

PREFATORY: 7
CHAPTER I — THE DOYLES ARE ASTONISHED 8
CHAPTER II — UNCLE JOHN MAKES PLANS...................................... 13
CHAPTER III — "ALL ASHORE".. 19
CHAPTER IV — SOME NEW ACQUAINTANCES, AND A WARNING 24
CHAPTER V — VESUVIUS RAMPANT 32
CHAPTER VI — UNDER A CLOUD 34
CHAPTER VII — A FRIEND IN NEED 40
CHAPTER VIII — ACROSS THE BAY 43
CHAPTER IX — COUNT FERRALTI 47
CHAPTER X — THE ROAD TO AMALFI 51
CHAPTER XI — THE EAGLE SCREAMS 58
CHAPTER XII — MOVING ON 63
CHAPTER XIII — IL DUCA 71
CHAPTER XIV — UNCLE JOHN DISAPPEARS.................................... 79
CHAPTER XV — DAYS OF ANXIETY 87
CHAPTER XVI — TATO.. 92
CHAPTER XVII — THE HIDDEN VALLEY 96
CHAPTER XVIII — GUESTS OF THE BRIGAND 102
CHAPTER XIX — A DIFFICULT POSITION 109
CHAPTER XX — UNCLE JOHN PLAYS EAVESDROPPER 115
CHAPTER XXI — THE PIT 121

CHAPTER XXII — NEWS AT LAST 126

CHAPTER XXIII — BETH BEGINS TO PLOT 132

CHAPTER XXIV — PATSY'S NEW FRIEND 136

CHAPTER XXV — TURNING THE TABLES 141

CHAPTER XXVI — THE COUNT UNMASKS 145

CHAPTER XXVII — TATO IS ADOPTED 150

CHAPTER XXVIII — DREAMS AND DRESS-MAKING 154

CHAPTER XXIX — TATO WINS 160

CHAPTER XXX — A WAY TO FORGET 165

— CHAPTER XXXI — SAFE HOME 169

PREFATORY:

The author is pleased to be able to present a sequel to "Aunt Jane's Nieces," the book which was received with so much favor last year. Yet it is not necessary one should have read the first book to fully understand the present volume, the characters being taken to entirely new scenes.

The various foreign localities are accurately described, so that those who have visited them will recognize them at once, while those who have not been so fortunate may acquire a clear conception of them. It was my good fortune to be an eye witness of the recent great eruption of Vesuvius.

Lest I be accused of undue sensationalism in relating the somewhat dramatic Sicilian incident, I will assure my reader that the story does not exaggerate present conditions in various parts of the island. In fact, Il Duca and Tato are drawn from life, although they did not have their mountain lair so near to Taormina as I have ventured to locate it. Except that I have adapted their clever system of brigandage to the exigencies of this story, their history is truly related. Many who have travelled somewhat outside the beaten tracks in Sicily will frankly vouch for this statement.

Italy is doing its best to suppress the Mafia and to eliminate brigandage from the beautiful islands it controls, but so few of the inhabitants are Italians or in sympathy with the government that the work of reformation is necessarily slow. Americans, especially, must exercise caution in travelling in any part of Sicily; yet with proper care not to tempt the irresponsible natives, they are as safe in Sicily as they are at home.

Aunt Jane's nieces are shown to be as frankly adventurous as the average clear headed American girl, but their experiences amid the environments of an ancient and still primitive civilization are in no wise extraordinary.

EDITH VAN DYNE.

CHAPTER I
THE DOYLES ARE ASTONISHED

It was Sunday afternoon in Miss Patricia Doyle's pretty flat at 3708 Willing Square. In the small drawing room Patricia--or Patsy, as she preferred to be called--was seated at the piano softly playing the one "piece" the music teacher had succeeded in drilling into her flighty head by virtue of much patience and perseverance. In a thick cushioned morris-chair reclined the motionless form of Uncle John, a chubby little man in a gray suit, whose features were temporarily eclipsed by the newspaper that was spread carefully over them. Occasionally a gasp or a snore from beneath the paper suggested that the little man was "snoozing" as he sometimes gravely called it, instead of listening to the music.

Major Doyle sat opposite, stiffly erect, with his admiring eyes full upon Patsy. At times he drummed upon the arms of his chair in unison with the music, nodding his grizzled head to mark the time as well as to emphasize his evident approbation. Patsy had played this same piece from start to finish seven times since dinner, because it was the only one she knew; but the Major could have listened to it seven hundred times without the flicker of an eyelash. It was not that he admired so much the "piece" the girl was playing as the girl who was playing the "piece." His pride in Patsy was unbounded. That she should have succeeded at all in mastering that imposing looking instrument--making it actually "play chunes"--was surely a thing to wonder at. But then, Patsy could do anything, if she but tried.

Suddenly Uncle John gave a dreadful snort and sat bolt upright, gazing at his companions with a startled look that melted into one of benign complacency as he observed his surroundings and realized where he was. The interruption gave Patsy an opportunity to stop playing the tune. She swung around on the stool and looked with amusement at her newly awakened uncle.

"You've been asleep," she said.

"No, indeed; quite a mistake," replied the little man, seriously. "I've only been thinking."

"An' such beautchiful thoughts," observed the Major, testily, for he resented the interruption of his Sunday afternoon treat. "You thought 'em aloud, sir, and the sound of it was a bad imithation of a bullfrog in a marsh. You'll have to give up eating the salad, sir."

"Bah! don't I know?" asked Uncle John, indignantly.

"Well, if your knowledge is better than our hearing, I suppose you do," retorted the Major. "But to an ignorant individual like meself the impression conveyed was that you snored like a man that has forgotten his manners an' gone to sleep in the presence of a lady."

"Then no one has a better right to do that," declared Patsy, soothingly; "and I'm sure our dear Uncle John's thoughts were just the most beautiful dreams in the world. Tell us of them, sir, and we'll prove the Major utterly wrong."

Even her father smiled at the girl's diplomacy, and Uncle John, who was on the verge of unreasonable anger, beamed upon her gratefully.

"I'm going to Europe," he said.

The Major gave an involuntary start, and then turned to look at him curiously.

"And I'm going to take Patsy along," he continued, with a mischievous grin.

The Major frowned.

"Conthrol yourself, sir, until you are fully awake," said he. "You're dreaming again."

Patsy swung her feet from side to side, for she was such a little thing that the stool raised her entirely off the floor. There was a thoughtful look on her round, freckled face, and a wistful one in her great blue eyes as the full meaning of Uncle John's abrupt avowal became apparent.

The Major was still frowning, but a half frightened expression had replaced the one of scornful raillery. For he, too, knew that his eccentric brother-in-law was likely to propose any preposterous thing, and then carry it out in spite of all opposition. But to take Patsy to Europe would be like pulling the Major's eye teeth or amputating his good right arm. Worse; far worse! It would mean taking the sunshine out of her old father's sky altogether, and painting it a grim, despairing gray.

But he resolved not to submit without a struggle.

"Sir," said he, sternly--he always called his brother-in-law "sir" when he was in a sarcastic or reproachful mood--"I've had an idea for some time that you were plotting mischief. You haven't looked me straight in the eye for a week, and you've twice been late to dinner. I will ask you to explain to us, sir, the brutal suggestion you have just advanced."

Uncle John laughed. In the days when Major Doyle had thought him a poor man and in need of a helping hand, the grizzled old Irishman had been as tender toward him as a woman and studiously avoided any speech or epithet that by chance might injure the feelings of his dead wife's only brother. But the Major's invariable courtesy to the poor or unfortunate was no longer in evidence when he found that John Merrick was a multi-millionaire with a strongly defined habit of doing good to others and striving in obscure and unconventional ways to make everybody around him happy. His affection for the little man increased mightily, but his respectful attitude promptly changed, and a chance to reprove or discomfit his absurdly rich brother-in-law was one of his most satisfactory diversions. Uncle John appreciated this, and holding the dignified Major in loving regard was glad to cross swords with him now and then to add variety to their pleasant relations.

"It's this way, Major Doyle," he now remarked, coolly. "I've been worried to death, lately, over business matters; and I need a change."

"Phoo! All your business is attended to by Isham, Marvin & Co. You've no worry at all. Why, we've just made you a quarter of a million in C.H. & D's."

The "we" is explained by stating that the Major held an important position in the great banking house--a position Mr. Merrick had secured for him some months previously.

"That's it!" said Uncle John. "You've made me a quarter of a million that I don't want. The C.H. & D. stocks were going to pieces when I bought them, and I had reason to hope I'd lose a good round sum on them. But the confounded luck turned, and the result is an accumulation of all this dreadful money. So, my dear Major, before I'm tempted to do some-other foolish thing I've determined to run away, where business can't follow me, and where by industry and perseverance I can scatter some of my ill-gotten gains."

The Major smiled grimly.

"That's Europe, right enough," he said. "And I don't object, John, to your going there whenever you please. You're disgracefully countryfied and uninformed for a man of means, and Europe'll open your eyes and prove to you how insignificant you really are. I advise you to visit Ireland, sor, which I'm reliably informed is the centhral jewel in Europe's crown of beauty. Go; and go whinever you please, sor; but forbear the wickedness of putting foolish thoughts into our Patsy's sweet head. She can't go a step, and you know it. It's positive cruelty to her, sir, to suggest such a thing!"

The Major's speech had a touch of the brogue when he became excited, but recovered when he calmed down.

"Why, you selfish old humbug!" cried Uncle John, indignantly. "Why can't she go, when there's money and time to spare? Would you keep her here to cuddle and spoil a vigorous man like yourself, when she can run away and see the world and be happy?"

"It's a great happiness to cuddle the Major," said Patsy, softly; "and the poor man needs it as much as he does his slippers or his oatmeal for breakfast."

"And Patsy has the house to look after," added the Major, complacently.

Uncle John gave a snort of contempt.

"For an unreasonable man, show me an Irishman," he remarked. "Here you've been telling me how Europe is an education and a delight, and in the next breath you deliberately deprive your little daughter, whom you pretend to love, of the advantages she might gain by a trip abroad! And why? Just because you want her yourself, and might be a bit lonesome without her. But I'll settle that foolishness, sir, in short order. You shall go with us."

"Impossible!" ejaculated the Major. "It's the time of year I'm most needed in the office, and Mr. Marvin has been so kind and considerate that I won't play him a dirty trick by leaving him in the lurch."

Patsy nodded approval.

"That's right, daddy," she said.

Uncle John lay back in the chair and put the newspaper over his face again. Patsy and her father stared at one another with grave intentness. Then the Major drew out his handkerchief and mopped his brow.

"You'd like to go, mavourneen?" he asked, softly.

"Yes, daddy; but I won't, of course."

"Tut-tut! don't you go putting yourself against your old father's will, Patsy. It's not so far to Europe," he continued, thoughtfully, "and you won't be away much longer than you were when you went to Elmhurst after Aunt

Jane's money--which you didn't get. Mary takes fine care of our little rooms, and doubtless I shall be so busy that I won't miss you at all, at all."

"Daddy!"

She was in his lap, now, her chubby arms clasped around his neck and her soft cheek laid close beside his rough and ruddy one.

"And when ye get back, Patsy darlin'," he whispered, tenderly stroking her hair, "the joy of the meeting will make up for all that we've suffered. It's the way of life, mavourneen. Unless a couple happens to be Siamese twins, they're bound to get separated in the course of events, more or less, if not frequently."

"I won't go, daddy."

"Oh, yes you will. It's not like you to be breakin' my heart by stayin' home. Next week, said that wicked old uncle--he remoinds me of the one that tried to desthroy the Babes in the Woods, Patsy dear. You must try to reclaim him to humanity, for I'm hopin' there's a bit of good in the old rascal yet." And he looked affectionately at the round little man under the newspaper.

Uncle John emerged again. It was wonderful how well he understood the Doyle family. His face was now smiling and wore a look of supreme satisfaction.

"Your selfishness, my dear Major," said he, "is like the husk on a cocoanut. When you crack it there's plenty of milk within--and in your case it's the milk of human kindness. Come! let's talk over the trip."

CHAPTER II
UNCLE JOHN MAKES PLANS

"The thought came to me a long time ago," Uncle John resumed; "but it was only yesterday that I got all the details fixed and settled in my mind. I've been a rough old duffer, Patsy, and in all my hard working life never thought of such a thing as travelling or enjoying myself until I fell in with you, and you taught me how pleasant it is to scatter sunshine in the hearts of others. For to make others happy means a lot of joy for yourself--a secret you were trying to keep from me, you crafty young woman, until I discovered it by accident. Now, here I am with three nieces on my hands--"

"You may say two, sir," interrupted the Major. "Patsy can take care of herself."

"Hold your tongue," said Uncle John. "I say I've got three nieces--as fine a trio of intelligent, sweet and attractive young women as you'll run across in a month of Sundays. I dare you to deny it, sir. And they are all at an age when an European trip will do them a world of good. So off we go, a week from Tuesday, in the first-class steamer 'Princess Irene,' bound from New York for the Bay of Naples!"

Patsy's eyes showed her delight. They fairly danced.

"Have you told Beth and Louise?" she asked.

His face fell.

"Not yet," he said. "I'd forgotten to mention it to them."

"For my part," continued the girl, "I can get ready in a week, easily. But Beth is way out in Ohio, and we don't know whether she can go or not."

"I'll telegraph her, and find out," said Uncle John.

"Do it to-day," suggested the Major.

"I will."

"And to-morrow you must see Louise," added Patsy. "I'm not sure she'll want to go, dear. She's such a social butterfly, you know, that her engagements may keep her at home."

"Do you mean to say she's engaged?" asked Mr. Merrick, aghast.

"Only for the parties and receptions, Uncle. But it wouldn't surprise me if she was married soon. She's older than Beth or me, and has a host of admirers."

"Perhaps she's old enough to be sensible," suggested the Major.

"Well, I'll see her and her mother to-morrow morning," decided Uncle John, "and if she can't find time for a trip to Europe at my expense, you and Beth shall go anyhow--and we'll bring Louise a wedding present."

With this declaration he took his hat and walking stick and started for the telegraph station, leaving Patsy and her father to canvass the unexpected situation.

John Merrick was sixty years old, but as hale and rugged as a boy of twenty. He had made his vast fortune on the Pacific Coast and during his years of busy activity had been practically forgotten by the Eastern members of his family, who never had credited him with sufficient ability to earn more than a precarious livelihood. But the man was shrewd enough in a business way, although simple almost to childishness in many other matters. When he returned, quite unheralded, to end his days "at home" and employ his ample wealth to the best advantage, he for a time kept his success a secret, and so learned much of the dispositions and personal characteristics of his three nieces.

They were at that time visiting his unmarried sister, Jane, at her estate at Elmhurst, whither they had been invited for the first time; and in the race for Aunt Jane's fortune he watched the three girls carefully and found much to admire in each one of them. Patsy Doyle, however, proved exceptionally frank and genuine, and when Aunt Jane at last died and it was found she had no estate to bequeath, Patsy proved the one bright star in the firmament of disappointment. Supposing Uncle John to be poor, she insisted upon carrying him to New York with her and sharing with him the humble tenement room in which she lived with her father--a retired veteran who helped pay the family expenses by keeping books for a mercantile firm, while Patsy worked in a hair-dresser's shop.

It was now that Uncle John proved a modern fairy godfather to Aunt Jane's nieces--who were likewise his own nieces. The three girls had little in common except their poverty, Elizabeth De Graf being the daughter of a music teacher, in Cloverton, Ohio, while Louise Merrick lived with her widowed mother in a social atmosphere of the second class in New York, where the two women frankly intrigued to ensnare for Louise a husband who had sufficient means to ensure both mother and daughter a comfortable home. In spite of this worldly and unlovely ambition, which their circumstances might partially excuse, Louise, who was but seventeen, had many good and womanly qualities, could they have been developed in an atmosphere uninfluenced by the schemes of her vain and selfish mother.

Uncle John, casting aside the mask of poverty, came to the relief of all three girls. He settled the incomes of substantial sums of money upon both Beth and Louise, making them practically independent. For Patsy he bought a handsome modern flat building located at 3708 Willing Square, and installed her and the Major in its cosiest apartment, the rents of the remaining flats giving the Doyles an adequate income for all time to come. Here Uncle John, believing himself cordially welcome, as indeed he was, made his own home, and it required no shrewd guessing to arrive at the conclusion that little Patsy was destined to inherit some day all his millions.

The great banking and brokerage firm of Isham, Marvin & Co. had long managed successfully John Merrick's vast fortune, and at his solicitation it gave Major Doyle a responsible position in its main office, with a salary that rendered him independent of his daughter's suddenly acquired wealth and made him proud and self-respecting.

Money had no power to change the nature of the Doyles. The Major remained the same simple, honest, courteous yet brusque old warrior who had won Uncle John's love as a hard working book-keeper; and Patsy's bright and sunny disposition had certain power to cheer any home, whether located in a palace or a hovel.

Never before in his life had Uncle John been so supremely happy, and never before had Aunt Jane's three nieces had so many advantages and pleasures. It was to confer still further benefits upon these girls that their eccentric uncle had planned this unexpected European trip.

His telegram to Elizabeth was characteristic:

"Patsy, Louise and I sail for Europe next Tuesday. Will you join us as my guest? If so, take first train to New York, where I will look after your outfit. Answer immediately."

That was a message likely to surprise a country girl, but it did not strike John Merrick as in any way extraordinary. He thought he could depend upon Beth. She would be as eager to go as he was to have her, and when he had paid for the telegram he dismissed the matter from further thought.

Next morning Patsy reminded him that instead of going down town he must personally notify Louise Merrick of the proposed trip; so he took a cross-town line and arrived at the Merrick's home at nine o'clock.

Mrs. Merrick was in a morning wrapper, sipping her coffee in an upper room. But she could not deny herself to Uncle John, her dead husband's brother and her only daughter's benefactor (which meant indirectly her own benefactor), so she ordered the maid to show him up at once.

"Louise is still sweetly sleeping," she said, "and won't waken for hours yet."

"Is anything wrong with her?" he asked, anxiously.

"Oh, dear, no! but everyone does not get up with the milkman, as you do, John; and the dear child was at the opera last night, which made her late in getting home."

"Doesn't the opera let out before midnight, the same as the theatres?" he asked.

"I believe so; but there is the supper, afterward, you know."

"Ah, yes," he returned, thoughtfully. "I've always noticed that the opera makes folks desperately hungry, for they flock to the restaurants as soon as they can get away. Singular, isn't it?"

"Why, I never thought of it in that light."

"But Louise is well?"

"Quite well, thank you."

"That's a great relief, for I'm going to take her to Europe with me next week," he said.

Mrs. Merrick was so astonished that she nearly dropped her coffee-cup and could make no better reply than to stare blankly at her brother-in-law.

"We sail Tuesday," continued Uncle John, "and you must have my niece ready in time and deliver her on board the 'Princess Irene' at Hoboken at nine o'clock, sharp."

"But John--John!" gasped Mrs. Merrick, feebly, "it will take a month, at least, to make her gowns, and--"

"Stuff and rubbish!" he growled. "That shows, Martha, how little you know about European trips. No one makes gowns to go abroad with; you buy 'em in Paris to bring home."

"Ah, yes; to be sure," she muttered. "Perhaps, then, it can be done, if Louise, has no other engagements."

"Just what Patsy said. See here, Martha, do you imagine that any girl who is half human could have engagements that would keep her from Europe?"

"But the requirements of society--"

"You'll get me riled, pretty soon, Martha; and if you do you'll wish you hadn't."

This speech frightened the woman. It wouldn't do to provoke Uncle John, however unreasonable he happened to be. So she said, meekly:

"I've no doubt Louise will be delighted to go, and so will I."

"You!"

"Why--why--whom do you intend taking?"

"Just the three girls--Aunt Jane's three nieces. Also mine."

"But you'll want a chaperone for them."

"Why so?"

"Propriety requires it; and so does ordinary prudence. Louise, I know, will be discreet, for it is her nature; but Patsy is such a little flyaway and Beth so deep and demure, that without a chaperone they might cause you a lot of trouble."

Uncle John grew red and his eyes flashed.

"A chaperone!" he cried, contemptuously; "not any in mine, Martha Merrick. Either we young folks go alone, without any death's head to perpetually glower at us, or we don't go at all! Three better girls never lived, and I'll trust 'em anywhere. Besides that, we aren't going to any of your confounded social functions; we're going on a reg'lar picnic, and if I don't give those girls the time of their lives my name ain't John Merrick. A chaperone, indeed!"

Mrs. Merrick held up her hands in horror.

"I'm not sure, John," she gasped, "that I ought to trust my dear child with an uncle who disregards so openly the proprieties."

"Well, I'm sure; and the thing's settled," he said, more calmly. "Don't worry, ma'am. I'll look after Patsy and Beth, and Louise will look after all of us--just as she does after you--because she's so discreet. Talk about your being a chaperone! Why, you don't dare say your soul's your own when Louise is awake. That chaperone business is all humbuggery--unless an old uncle like me can be a chaperone. Anyhow, I'm the only one that's going to be appointed. I won't wait for Louise to wake up. Just tell her the news and help her to get ready on time. And now, I'm off. Good morning, Martha."

She really had no words of protest ready at hand, and it was long after queer old John Merrick had gone away that she remembered a dozen effective speeches that she might have delivered.

"After all," she sighed, taking up her cup again, "it may be the best thing in the world for Louise. We don't know whether that young Weldon, who is paying her attentions just now, is going to inherit his father's money or not. He's been a bit wild, I've heard, and it is just as well to postpone any engagement until we find out the facts. I can do that nicely while my sweet child is in Europe with Uncle John, and away from all danger of entanglements. Really, it's an ill wind that blows no good! I'll go talk with Louise."

CHAPTER III
"ALL ASHORE"

Beth De Graf was a puzzle to all who knew her. She was a puzzle even to herself, and was wont to say, indifferently, that the problem was not worth a solution. For this beautiful girl of fifteen was somewhat bitter and misanthropic, a condition perhaps due to the uncongenial atmosphere in which she had been reared. She was of dark complexion and her big brown eyes held a sombre and unfathomable expression. Once she had secretly studied their reflection in a mirror, and the eyes awed and frightened her, and made her uneasy. She had analyzed them much as if they belonged to someone else, and wondered what lay behind their mask, and what their capabilities might be.

But this morbid condition mostly affected her when she was at home, listening to the unpleasant bickerings of her father and mother, who quarrelled constantly over trifles that Beth completely ignored. Her parents seemed like two ill tempered animals confined in the same cage, she thought, and their snarls had long since ceased to interest her.

This condition had, of course, been infinitely worse in all those dreadful years when they were poverty stricken. Since Uncle John had settled a comfortable income on his niece the grocer was paid promptly and Mrs. De Graf wore a silk dress on Sundays and held her chin a little higher than any other of the Cloverton ladies dared do. The Professor, no longer harrassed by debts, devoted less time to the drudgery of teaching and began the composition of an oratorio that he firmly believed would render his name famous. So, there being less to quarrel about, Beth's parents indulged more moderately in that pastime; but their natures were discordant, and harmony in the De Graf household was impossible.

When away from home Beth's disposition softened. Some of her schoolfriends had seen her smile--a wonderful and charming phenomenon, during which her expression grew sweet and bewitchingly animated and her brown eyes radiant with mirthful light. It was not the same Beth at all.

Sometimes, when the nieces were all at Aunt Jane's, Beth had snuggled in the arms of her cousin Louise, who had a way of rendering herself agreeable to all with whom she came in contact, and tried hard to win the affection of the frankly antagonistic girl. At such times the gentleness of Elizabeth, her almost passionate desire to be loved and fondled, completely transformed her for the moment. Louise, shrewd at reading others, told herself that Beth possessed a reserve force of tenderness, amiability and fond devotion that would render her adorable if she ever allowed those qualities full expression. But she did not tell Beth that. The girl was so accustomed to despise herself and so suspicious of any creditable impulses that at times unexpectedly obtruded themselves, that she would have dismissed such a suggestion as arrant flattery, and Louise was clever enough not to wish to arouse her cousin to a full consciousness of her own possibilities.

The trained if not native indifference of this strange girl of fifteen was demonstrated by her reception of Uncle John's telegram. She quietly handed it to her mother and said, as calmly as if it were an invitation to a church picnic:

"I think I shall go."

"Nothing like that ever happened to me," remarked Mrs. De Graf, enviously. "If John Merrick had an atom of common sense he'd have taken me to Europe instead of a troop of stupid school girls. But John always was a fool, and always will be. When will you start, Beth?"

"To-morrow morning. There's nothing to keep me. I'll go to Patsy and stay with her until we sail."

"Are you glad?" asked her mother, looking into the expressionless face half curiously.

"Yes," returned Beth, as if considering her reply; "a change is always interesting, and I have never travelled except to visit Aunt Jane at Elmhurst. So I think I am pleased to go to Europe."

Mrs. De Graf sighed. There was little in common between mother and daughter; but that, to a grave extent, was the woman's fault. She had never tried to understand her child's complex nature, and somewhat resented Beth's youth and good looks, which she considered contrasted unfavorably with her own deepening wrinkles and graying hair. For Mrs. De Graf was vain and self-important, and still thought herself attractive and even girlish. It would really be a relief to have Beth out of the way for a few months.

The girl packed her own trunk and arranged for it to be taken to the station. In the morning she entered the music room to bid the Professor good-bye. He frowned at the interruption, for the oratorio was especially engrossing at the time. Mrs. De Graf kissed her daughter lightly upon the lips and said in a perfunctory way that she hoped Beth would have a good time.

The girl had no thought of resenting the lack of affection displayed by her parents. It was what she had always been accustomed to, and she had no reason to expect anything different.

Patsy met her at the train in New York and embraced her rapturously. Patsy was really fond of Beth; but it was her nature to be fond of everyone, and her cousin, escaping from her smacking and enthusiastic kisses, told herself that Patsy would have embraced a cat with the same spontaneous ecstacy. That was not strictly true, but there was nothing half hearted or halfway about Miss Doyle. If she loved you, there would never be an occasion for you to doubt the fact. It was Patsy's way.

Uncle John also was cordial in his greetings. He was very proud of his pretty niece, and discerning enough to realize there was a broad strata of womanliness somewhere in Elizabeth's undemonstrative character. He had promised himself to "dig it out" some day, and perhaps the European trip would give him his opportunity.

Patsy and Elizabeth shopped for the next few days most strenuously and delightfully. Sometimes their dainty cousin Louise joined them, and the three girls canvassed gravely their requirements for a trip that was as new to them as a flight to the moon. Naturally, they bought much that was unnecessary and forgot many things that would have been useful. You have to go twice to Europe to know what to take along.

Louise needed less than the others, for her wardrobe was more extensive and she already possessed all that a young girl could possibly make use of. This niece, the eldest of Uncle John's trio, was vastly more experienced in the ways of the world than the others, although as a traveller she had no advantage of them. Urged thereto by her worldly mother, she led a sort of trivial, butterfly existence, and her character was decidedly superficial to any close observer. Indeed, her very suavity and sweetness of manner was assumed, because it was so much more comfortable and effective to be agreeable than otherwise. She was now past seventeen years of age, tall and well formed, with a delicate and attractive face which, without being beautiful, was considered pleasant and winning. Her eyes were good, though a bit too shrewd, and her light brown hair was fluffy as spun silk. Graceful of carriage, gracious of manner, yet affecting a languor unsuited to her years, Louise Merrick was a girl calculated to draw from the passing throng glances of admiration and approval, and to convey the impression of good breeding and feminine cleverness.

All this, however, was outward. Neither Patsy nor Beth displayed any undue affection for their cousin, although all of the girls exhibited a fair amount of cousinly friendship for one another. They had once been thrown together under trying circumstances, when various qualities of temperament not altogether admirable were liable to assert themselves. Those events were too recent to be already forgotten, yet the girls were generous enough to be considerate of each others' failings, and had resolved to entertain no sentiment other than good will on the eve of their departure for such a charming outing as Uncle John had planned for them.

Mr. Merrick being a man, saw nothing radically wrong in the dispositions of any of his nieces. Their youth and girlishness appealed to him strongly, and he loved to have them by his side. It is true that he secretly regretted Louise was not more genuine, that Beth was so cynical and frank, and that Patsy was not more diplomatic. But he reflected that he had had no hand in molding their characters, although he might be instrumental in improving them; so he accepted the girls as they were, thankful that their faults were not glaring, and happy to have found three such interesting nieces to cheer his old age.

At last the preparations were complete. Tuesday arrived, and Uncle John "corralled his females," as he expressed it, and delivered them safely on board the staunch and comfortable ocean greyhound known as the "Princess Irene," together with their bags and baggage, their flowers and fruits and candy boxes and all those other useless accessories to a voyage so eagerly thrust upon the departing travellers by their affectionate but ill-advised friends.

Mrs. Merrick undertook the exertion of going to Hoboken to see her daughter off, and whispered in the ear of Louise many worldly admonitions and such bits of practical advice as she could call to mind on the spur of the moment.

Major Gregory Doyle was there, pompous and straight of form and wearing an assumed smile that was meant to assure Patsy he was delighted at her going, but which had the effect of scaring the girl because she at first thought the dreadful expression was due to convulsions.

The Major had no admonitions for Patsy, but she had plenty for him, and gave him a long list of directions that would, as he said, cause him to "walk mighty sthraight" if by good luck he managed to remember them all.

Having made up his mind to let the child go to Europe, the old fellow allowed no wails or bemoanings to reach Patsy's ears to deprive her of a moment's joyful anticipation of the delights in store for her. He laughed and joked perpetually during that last day, and promised the girl that he would take a vacation while she was gone and visit his old colonel in Virginia, which she knew was the rarest pleasure he could enjoy. And now he stood upon the deck amusing them all with his quaint sayings and appearing so outwardly jolly and unaffected that only Patsy herself suspected the deep grief that was gripping his kindly old heart.

Uncle John guessed, perhaps, for he hugged the Major in a tight embrace, whispering that Patsy should be now, as ever, the apple of his eye and the subject of his most loving care.

"An' don't be forgetting to bring me the meerschaum pipe from Sicily an' the leathern pocket-book from Florence," the Major said to Patsy, impressively. "It's little enough for ye to remember if ye go that way, an' to tell the truth I'm sending ye abroad just for to get them. An' don't be gettin' off the boat till it stops at a station; an' remember that Uncle John is full of rheumatics an' can't walk more n' thirty mile an hour, an'--"

"It's a slander," said Uncle John, stoutly. "I never had rheumatics in my life."

"Major," observed Patsy, her blue eyes full of tears but her lips trying to smile, "do have the tailor sponge your vest every Saturday. It's full of spots even now, and I've been too busy lately to look after you properly. You're--you're--just disgraceful, Major!"

"All ashore!" called a loud voice.

The Major gathered Patsy into an embrace that threatened to crush her, and then tossed her into Uncle John's arms and hurried away. Mrs. Merrick followed, with good wishes for all for a pleasant journey; and then the four voyagers pressed to the rail and waved their handkerchiefs frantically to those upon the dock while the band played vociferously and the sailors ran here and there in sudden excitement and the great ship left her moorings and moved with proud deliberation down the bay to begin her long voyage to Gibraltar and the blue waters of the Mediterranean.

CHAPTER IV
SOME NEW ACQUAINTANCES, AND A WARNING

For an inexperienced tourist Uncle John managed their arrangements most admirably. He knew nothing at all about ocean travel or what was the proper method to secure comfortable accommodations; but while most of the passengers were writing hurried letters in the second deck gallery, which were to be sent back by the pilot, Mr. Merrick took occasion to interview the chief steward and the deck steward and whatever other official he could find, and purchased their good will so liberally that the effect of his astute diplomacy was immediately apparent.

His nieces found that the sunniest deck chairs bore their names; the most desirable seats in the dining hall were theirs when, half famished because breakfast had been disregarded, they trooped in to luncheon; the best waiters on the ship attended to their wants, and afterward their cabins were found to be cosily arranged with every comfort the heart of maid could wish for.

At luncheon it was found that the steward had placed a letter before Uncle John's plate. The handwriting of the address Louise, who sat next her uncle, at once recognized as that of her mother; but she said nothing.

Mr. Merrick was amazed at the contents of the communication, especially as he had so recently parted with the lady who had written it.

It said: "I must warn you, John, that my daughter has just escaped a serious entanglement, and I am therefore more grateful than I can express that you are taking her far from home for a few weeks. A young man named Arthur Weldon--a son of the big railroad president, you know--has been paying Louise marked attentions lately; but I cautioned her not to encourage him because a rumor had reached me that he has quarrelled with his father and been disinherited. My informant also asserted that the young man is wild and headstrong and cannot be controlled by his parent; but he always seemed gentlemanly enough at our house, and my greatest objection to him is that he is not likely to inherit a dollar of his father's money. Louise and I decided to keep him dangling until we could learn the truth of this matter, for you can easily understand that with her exceptional attractions there is no object in Louise throwing herself away upon a poor man, or one who cannot give her a prominent position in society. Imagine my horror, John, when I discovered last evening that my only child, whom I have so fondly cherished, has ungratefully deceived me. Carried away by the impetuous avowals of this young scapegrace, whom his own father disowns, she has confessed her love for him--love for a pauper!--and only by the most stringent exercise of my authority have I been able to exact from Louise a promise that she will not become formally engaged to Arthur Weldon, or even correspond with him, until she has returned home. By that time I shall have learned more of his history and prospects, when I can better decide whether to allow the affair to go on. Of course I have hopes that in case my fears are proven to have been well founded, I can arouse Louise to a proper spirit and induce her to throw the fellow over. Meantime, I implore you, as my daughter's temporary guardian, not to allow Louise to speak of or dwell upon this young man, but try to interest her in other gentlemen whom you may meet and lead her to forget, if possible, her miserable entanglement. Consider a loving mother's feelings, John. Try to help me in this emergency, and I shall be forever deeply grateful."

"It's from mother, isn't it?" asked Louise, when he had finished reading the letter.

"Yes," he answered gruffly, as he crumpled the missive and stuffed it into his pocket.

"What does she say, Uncle?"

"Nothing but rubbish and nonsense. Eat your soup, my dear; it's getting cold."

The girl's sweet, low laughter sounded very pleasant, and served to calm his irritation. From her demure yet amused expression Uncle John guessed that Louise knew the tenor of her mother's letter as well as if she had read it over his shoulder, and it comforted him that she could take the matter so lightly. Perhaps the poor child was not so deeply in love as her mother had declared.

He was greatly annoyed at the confidence Mrs. Merrick had seen fit to repose in him, and felt she had no right to burden him with any knowledge of such an absurd condition of affairs just as he was starting for a holiday.

Whatever might be the truth of the girl's "entanglement,"--and he judged that it was not all conveyed in Martha Merrick's subtle letter--Louise would surely be free and unhampered by either love or maternal diplomacy for some time to come. When she returned home her mother might conduct the affair to suit herself. He would have nothing to do with it in any way.

As soon as luncheon was finished they rushed for the deck, and you may imagine that chubby little Uncle John, with his rosy, smiling face and kindly eyes, surrounded by three eager and attractive girls of from fifteen to seventeen years of age, was a sight to compel the attention of every passenger aboard the ship.

It was found easy to make the acquaintance of the interesting group, and many took advantage of that fact; for Uncle John chatted brightly with every man and Patsy required no excuse of a formal introduction to confide to every woman that John Merrick was taking his three nieces to Europe to "see the sights and have the time of their lives."

Many of the business men knew well the millionaire's name, and accorded him great respect because he was so enormously wealthy and successful. But the little man was so genuinely human and unaffected and so openly scorned all toadyism that they soon forgot his greatness in the financial world and accepted him simply as a good fellow and an invariably cheerful comrade.

The weather was somewhat rough for the latter part of March--they had sailed the twenty-seventh--but the "Irene" was so staunch and rode the waves so gracefully that none of the party except Louise was at all affected by the motion. The eldest cousin, however, claimed to be indisposed for the first few days out, and so Beth and Patsy and Uncle John sat in a row in their steamer chairs, with the rugs tucked up to their waists, and kept themselves and everyone around them merry and light hearted.

Next to Patsy reclined a dark complexioned man of about thirty-five, with a long, thin face and intensely black, grave eyes. He was carelessly dressed and wore a flannel shirt, but there was an odd look of mingled refinement and barbarity about him that arrested the girl's attention. He sat very quietly in his chair, reserved both in speech and in manner; but when she forced him to talk he spoke impetuously and with almost savage emphasis, in a broken dialect that amused her immensely.

"You can't be American," she said.

"I am Sicilian," was the proud answer.

"That's what I thought; Sicilian or Italian or Spanish; but I'm glad it's Sicilian, which is the same as Italian. I can't speak your lingo myself," she continued, "although I am studying it hard; but you manage the English pretty well, so we shall get along famously together."

He did not answer for a moment, but searched her unconscious face with his keen eyes. Then he demanded, brusquely:

"Where do you go?"

"Why, to Europe," she replied, as if surprised.

"Europe? Pah! It is no answer at all," he responded, angrily. "Europe is big. To what part do you journey?"

Patsy hesitated. The magic word "Europe" had seemed to sum up their destination very effectively, and she had heretofore accepted it as sufficient, for the time being, at least. Uncle John had bought an armful of guide books and Baedeckers, but in the hurry of departure she had never glanced inside them. To go to Europe had been enough to satisfy her so far, but perhaps she should have more definite knowledge concerning their trip. So she turned to Uncle John and said:

"Uncle, dear, to what part of Europe are we going?"

"What part?" he answered. "Why, it tells on the ticket, Patsy. I can't remember the name just now. It's where the ship stops, of course."

"That is Napoli," said the thin faced man, with a scarcely veiled sneer. "And then?"

"And then?" repeated Patsy, turning to her Uncle.

"Then? Oh, some confounded place or other that I can't think of. I'm not a time-table, Patsy; but the trip is all arranged, in beautiful style, by a friend of mine who has always wanted to go abroad, and so has the whole programme mapped out in his head."

"Is it in his head yet?" enquired Patsy, anxiously.

"No, dear; it's in the left hand pocket of my blue coat, all written down clearly. So what's the use of bothering? We aren't there yet. By and bye we'll get to Eu-rope an' do it up brown. Whatever happens, and wherever we go, it's got to be a spree and a jolly good time; so take it easy, Patsy dear, and don't worry."

"That's all right, Uncle," she rejoined, with a laugh. "I'm not worrying the least mite. But when folks ask us where we're going, what shall we say?"

"Eu-rope."

"And then?" mischievously.

"And then home again, of course. It's as plain as the nose on your face, Patsy Doyle, and a good bit straighter."

That made her laugh again, and the strange Italian, who was listening, growled a word in his native language. He wasn't at all a pleasant companion, but for that very reason Patsy determined to make him talk and "be sociable." By degrees he seemed to appreciate her attention, and always brightened when she came to sit beside him.

"You'll have to tell me your name, you know," she said to him; "because I can't be calling you 'Sir' every minute."

He glanced nervously around. Then he answered, slowly:

"I am called Valdi--Victor Valdi."

"Oh, that's a pretty name, Mr. Valdi--or should I say Signor?"

"You should."

"Do I pronounce it right?"

"No."

"Well, never mind if I don't; you'll know what I mean, and that I intend to be proper and polite," she responded, sweetly.

Beth, while she made fewer acquaintances than Patsy, seemed to have cast off her sullen reserve when she boarded the ship. In truth, the girl was really happy for the first time in her life, and it softened her so wonderfully and made her so attractive that she soon formed a select circle around her. A young lady from Cleveland, who had two big brothers, was impelled to introduce herself to Beth because of the young men's intense admiration for the girl's beautiful face. When it was found that they were all from Ohio, they formed a friendly alliance at once. Marion Horton was so frank and agreeable that she managed to draw out all that was best in Beth's nature, and the stalwart young Hortons were so shyly enthusiastic over this, their first trip abroad, that they inspired the girl with a like ardor, which resulted in the most cordial relations between them.

And it so happened that several other young men who chanced to be aboard the "Princess Irene" marked the Hortons' intimacy with Beth and insisted on being introduced by them, so that by the time Louise had conquered her mal-de-mer and appeared on deck, she found an admiring group around her cousin that included most of the desirable young fellows on the ship. Beth sat enthroned like a queen, listening to her courtiers and smiling encouragement now and then, but taking little part in the conversation herself because of her inexperience. Such adoration was new to the little country girl, and she really enjoyed it. Nor did the young men resent her silence. All that they wanted her to do, as Tom Horton tersely expressed it, was to "sit still and look pretty."

As for Uncle John, he was so delighted with Beth's social success that he adopted all the boys on the spot, and made them a part of what he called his family circle.

Louise, discovering this state of affairs, gave an amused laugh and joined the group. She was a little provoked that she had isolated herself so long in her cabin when there was interesting sport on deck; but having lost some valuable time she straightway applied herself to redeem the situation.

In the brilliance of her conversation, in her studied glances, in a thousand pretty ways that were skillfully rendered effective, she had a decided advantage over her more beautiful cousin. When Louise really desired to please she was indeed a charming companion, and young men are not likely to detect insincerity in a girl who tries to captivate them.

The result was astonishing to Uncle John and somewhat humiliating to Beth; for a new queen was presently crowned, and Louise by some magnetic power assembled the court around herself. Only the youngest Horton boy, in whose susceptible heart Beth's image was firmly enshrined, refused to change his allegiance; but in truth the girl enjoyed herself more genuinely in the society of one loyal cavalier than when so many were clamoring for her favors. The two would walk the deck together for hours without exchanging a single word, or sit together silently listening to the band or watching the waves, without the need, as Tom expressed it, of "jabbering every blessed minute" in order to be happy.

Patsy was indignant at the artfulness of Louise until she noticed that Beth was quite content; then she laughed softly and watched matters take their course, feeling a little sorry for the boys because she knew Louise was only playing with them.

The trip across the Atlantic was all too short. On the fifth of April they passed the Azores, running close to the islands of Fayal and San Jorge so that the passengers might admire the zigzag rows of white houses that reached from the shore far up the steep hillsides. On the sixth day they sighted Gibraltar and passed between the Moorish and Spanish lighthouses into the lovely waters of the Mediterranean. The world-famed rock was now disclosed to their eyes, and when the ship anchored opposite it Uncle John assisted his nieces aboard the lighter and took them for a brief excursion ashore.

Of course they rode to the fortress and wandered through its gloomy, impressive galleries, seeing little of the armament because visitors are barred from the real fortifications. The fortress did not seem especially impregnable and was, taken altogether, a distinct disappointment to them; but the ride through the town in the low basket phaetons was wholly delightful. The quaint, narrow streets and stone arches, the beautiful vistas of sea and mountain, the swarthy, dark-eyed Moors whose presence lent to the town an oriental atmosphere, and the queer market-places crowded with Spaniards, Frenchmen, Jews and red-coated English soldiers, altogether made up a panorama that was fascinating in the extreme.

But their stay was short, and after a rush of sightseeing that almost bewildered them they returned to the ship breathless but elated at having "seen an' done," as Uncle John declared, their first foreign port.

And now through waters so brightly blue and transparent that they aroused the girls' wonder and admiration, the good ship plowed her way toward the port of Naples, passing to the east of Sardinia and Corsica, which they viewed with eager interest because these places had always seemed so far away to them, and had now suddenly appeared as if by magic directly before their eyes.

Patsy and the big whiskered captain had become such good friends that he always welcomed the girl on his own exclusive deck, and this afternoon she sat beside him and watched the rugged panorama slip by.

"When will we get to Naples?" she asked.

"To-morrow evening, probably," answered the captain. "See, it is over in that direction, where the gray cloud appears in the sky."

"And what is the gray cloud, Captain?"

"I do not know," said he, gravely. "Perhaps smoke from Vesuvius. At Gibraltar we heard that the volcano is in an ugly mood, I hope it will cause you no inconvenience."

"Wouldn't it be fine if we could see an eruption!" exclaimed the girl.

The captain shook his head.

"Interesting, perhaps," he admitted; "but no great calamity that causes thousands of people to suffer can be called 'fine.'"

"Ah, that is true!" she said, quickly. "I had forgotten the suffering."

Next morning all the sky was thick with smoke, and the sun was hidden. The waters turned gray, too, and as they approached the Italian coast the gloom perceptibly increased. A feeling of uneasiness seemed to pervade the ship, and even the captain had so many things to consider that he had no time to converse with his little friend.

Signor Valdi forsook his deck chair for the first time and stood at the rail which overlooked the steerage with his eyes glued to the grim skies ahead. When Uncle John asked him what he saw he answered, eagerly:

"Death and destruction, and a loss of millions of lira to the bankrupt government. I know; for I have studied Etna for years, and Vesuvio is a second cousin to Etna."

"Hm," said Uncle John. "You seem pleased with the idea of an eruption."

The thin faced man threw a shrewd look from his dark eyes and smiled. Uncle John frowned at the look and stumped away. He was not at all easy in his own mind. He had brought three nieces for a holiday to this foreign shore, and here at the outset they were confronted by an intangible danger that was more fearful because it was not understood. It was enough to make his round face serious, although he had so strong an objection to unnecessary worry.

Afternoon tea was served on deck amidst an unusual quiet. People soberly canvassed the situation and remarked upon the fact that the darkness increased visibly as they neared the Bay of Naples. Beth couldn't drink her tea, for tiny black atoms fell through the air and floated upon the surface of the liquid. Louise retired to her stateroom with a headache, and found her white serge gown peppered with particles of lava dust which had fallen from the skies.

The pilot guided the ship cautiously past Capri and into the bay. The air was now black with volcanic dross and a gloom as of midnight surrounded them on every side. The shore, the mountain and the water of the bay itself were alike invisible.

CHAPTER V
VESUVIUS RAMPANT

It was Saturday night, the seventh day of April, nineteen hundred and six--a night never to be forgotten by those aboard the ship; a night which has its place in history.

At dinner the captain announced that he had dropped anchor at the Immacollatella Nuova, but at a safe distance from the shore, and that no passengers would be landed under any circumstances until the fall of ashes ceased and he could put his people ashore in a proper manner.

A spirit of unrest fell upon them all. Big Tom Horton whispered to Beth that he did not intend to leave her side until all danger was over. The deck was deserted, all the passengers crowding into the smoking room and saloons to escape the lava dust.

Few kept their rooms or ventured to sleep. At intervals a loud detonation from the volcano shook the air, and the mystery and awe of the enveloping gloom were so palpable as almost to be felt.

Toward midnight the wind changed, driving the cloud of ashes to the southward and sufficiently clearing the atmosphere to allow the angry glow of the crater to be distinctly seen. Now it shot a pillar of fire thousands of feet straight into the heavens; then it would darken and roll skyward great clouds that were illumined by the showers of sparks accompanying them.

The windows of every cabin facing the volcano were filled with eager faces, and in the smoking room Uncle John clasped Beth around the waist with one arm and Patsy with the other and watched the wonderful exhibition through the window with a grave and anxious face. Tom Horton had taken a position at one side of them and the dark Italian at the other. The latter assured Patsy they were in no danger whatever. Tom secretly hoped they were, and laid brave plans for rescuing Beth or perishing at her side. Louise chose to lie in her berth and await events with calm resignation. If they escaped she would not look haggard and hollow-eyed when morning came. If a catastrophy was pending she would have no power to prevent it.

It was four o'clock on Sunday morning when Vesuvius finally reached the climax of her travail. With a deep groan of anguish the mountain burst asunder, and from its side rolled a great stream of molten lava that slowly spread down the slope, consuming trees, vineyards and dwellings in its path and overwhelming the fated city of Bosco-Trecase.

Our friends marked the course of destruction by watching the thread of fire slowly wander down the mountain slope. They did not know of the desolation it was causing, but the sight was terrible enough to inspire awe in every breast.

The volcano was easier after that final outburst, but the black clouds formed thicker than ever, and soon obscured the sky again.

CHAPTER VI
UNDER A CLOUD

"After all," said Uncle John, next morning, "we may consider ourselves very lucky. Your parents might have come to Naples a hundred times, my dears, and your children may come a hundred times more, and yet never see the sights that have greeted us on our arrival. If the confounded old hill was bound to spout, it did the fair thing by spouting when we were around. Eh, Patsy?"

"I quite agree with you," said the girl. "I wouldn't have missed it for anything--if it really had to behave so."

"But you'll pay for it!" growled Signor Valdi, who had overheard these remarks. "You will pay for it with a thousand discomforts--and I'm glad that is so. Vesuvio is hell let loose; and it amuses you. Hundreds are lying dead and crushed; and you are lucky to be here. Listen," he dropped his voice to a whisper: "if these Neapolitans could see the rejoicing in my heart, they would kill me. And you? Pah! you are no better. You also rejoice--and they will welcome you to Naples. I have advice. Do not go on shore. It is useless."

They were all startled by this strange speech, and the reproof it conveyed made them a trifle uncomfortable; but Uncle John whispered that the man was mad, and to pay no attention to him.

Although ashes still fell softly upon the ship the day had somewhat lightened the gloom and they could see from deck the dim outlines of the shore. A crowd of boats presently swarmed around them, their occupants eagerly clamoring for passengers to go ashore, or offering fruits, flowers and souvenirs to any who might be induced to purchase. Their indifference to their own and their city's danger was astonishing. It was their custom to greet arriving steamers in this way, for by this means they gained a livelihood. Nothing short of absolute destruction seemed able to interfere with their established occupations.

A steam tender also came alongside, and after a cordial farewell to the ship's officers and their travelling acquaintances, Uncle John placed his nieces and their baggage aboard the tender, which shortly deposited them safely upon the dock.

Perhaps a lot of passengers more dismal looking never before landed on the beautiful shores of Naples--beautiful no longer, but presenting an appearance gray and grewsome. Ashes were ankle deep in the streets--a fine, flour-like dust that clung to your clothing, filled your eyes and lungs and seemed to penetrate everywhere. The foliage of the trees and shrubbery drooped under its load and had turned from green to the all-pervading gray. The grass was covered; the cornices and balconies of the houses were banked with ashes.

"Bless me!" said Uncle John. "It's as bad as Pompey, or whatever that city was called that was buried in the Bible days."

"Oh, not quite, Uncle," answered Patsy, in her cheery voice; "but it may be, before Vesuvius is satisfied."

"It is certainly bad enough," observed Louise, pouting as she marked the destruction of her pretty cloak by the grimy deposit that was fast changing its color and texture.

"Well, let us get under shelter as soon as possible," said Uncle John.

The outlines of a carriage were visible a short distance away. He walked up to the driver and said:

"We want to go to a hotel."

The man paid no attention.

"Ask him how much he charges, Uncle. You know you mustn't take a cab in Naples without bargaining."

"Why not?"

"The driver will swindle you."

"I'll risk that," he answered. "Just now we're lucky if we get a carriage at all." He reached up and prodded the jehu in the ribs with his cane. "How much to the Hotel Vesuvius?" he demanded, loudly.

The man woke up and flourished his whip, at the same time bursting into a flood of Italian.

The girls listened carefully. They had been trying to study Italian from a small book Beth had bought entitled "Italian in Three Weeks without a Master," but not a word the driver of the carriage said seemed to have occurred in the vocabulary of the book. He repeated "Vesuvio" many times, however, with scornful, angry or imploring intonations, and Louise finally said:

"He thinks you want to go to the volcano, Uncle. The hotel is the Vesuve, not the Vesuvius."

"What's the difference?"

"I don't know."

"All right; you girls just hop in, and leave the rest to me."

He tumbled them all into the vehicle, bag and baggage, and then said sternly to the driver:

"Ho-tel Ve-suve--Ve-suve--ho-tel Ve-suve! Drive there darned quick, or I'll break your confounded neck."

The carriage started. It plowed its way jerkily through the dust-laden streets and finally stopped at an imposing looking structure. The day was growing darker, and an electric lamp burned before the entrance. But no one came out to receive them.

Uncle John climbed out and read the sign. "Hotel du Vesuve." It was the establishment he had been advised to stop at while in Naples. He compared the sign with a card which he drew from his pocket, and knew that he had made no mistake.

Entering the spacious lobby, he found it deserted. In the office a man was hastily making a package of some books and papers and did not respond or even look up when spoken to. At the concierge's desk a big, whiskered man sat staring straight ahead of him with a look of abject terror in his eyes.

"Good morning," said Uncle John. "Fine day, isn't it?"

"Did you hear it?" whispered the concierge, as a dull boom, like that of a distant cannon, made the windows rattle in their casements.

"Of course," replied Mr. Merrick, carelessly. "Old Vesuve seems on a rampage. But never mind that now. We've just come from America, where the mountains are more polite, and we're going to stop at your hotel."

The concierge's eyes wandered from the man to the three girls who had entered and grouped themselves behind him. Then they fell upon the driver of the carriage, who burst into a torrent of vociferous but wholly unintelligible exclamations which Uncle John declared "must be an excuse--and a mighty poor one--for talking."

The whiskered man, whose cap was elaborately embroidered in gold with the words "Hotel du Vesuve," seemed to understand the driver. He sighed drearily and said to Mr. Merrick:

"You must pay him thirty lira."

"How much is that?"

"Six dollars."

"Not by a jugfull!"

"You made no bargain."

"I couldn't. He can't talk."

"He claims it is you who cannot talk."

"What!"

"And prices are advanced during these awful days. What does it matter? Your money will do you no good when we are all buried deep in ash and scoria."

The big man shuddered at this gloomy picture, and added, listlessly: "You'll have to pay."

Uncle John paid, but the driver wouldn't accept American money. The disconsolate concierge would, though. He unlocked a drawer, put the six dollars into one section and drew from another two ten-lira notes. The driver took them, bowed respectfully to the whiskered man, shot a broadside of invective Italian at the unconscious Americans, and left the hotel.

"How about rooms?" asked Uncle John.

"Take any you please," answered the concierge. "All our guests are gone but two--two mad Americans like yourselves. The servants are also gone; the chef has gone; the elevator conductors are gone. If you stay you'll have to walk up."

"Where have they all gone?" asked Uncle John, wonderingly.

"Fled, sir; fled to escape destruction. They remember Pompeii. Only Signor Floriano, the proprietor, and myself are left. We stick to the last. We are brave."

"So I see. Now, look here, my manly hero. It's possible we shall all live through it; I'll bet you a thousand to ten that we do. And then you'll be glad to realize you've pocketed a little more American money. Come out of that box and show us some rooms, and I'll help to build up your fortune."

The concierge obeyed. Even the horrors of the situation could not eliminate from his carefully trained nature that desire to accumulate which is the prime qualification of his profession. The Americans walked up one flight and found spacious rooms on the first floor, of which they immediately took possession.

"Send for our trunks," said Mr. Merrick; and the man consented to do so provided he could secure a proper vehicle.

"You will be obliged to pay high for it," he warned; "but that will not matter. To witness the destruction of our beautiful Naples is an unusual sight. It will be worth your money."

"We'll settle that in the dim hereafter," replied Uncle John. "You get the trunks, and I'll take care of the finances."

When the concierge had retired the girls began to stuff newspapers into the cracks of the windows of their sitting room, where the fine ash was sifting in and forming little drifts several inches in thickness. Also the atmosphere of the room was filled with impalpable particles of dust, which rendered breathing oppressive and unpleasant.

Uncle John watched them for a time, and his brow clouded.

"See here, girls," he exclaimed; "let's hold a council of war. Do you suppose we are in any real danger?"

They grouped around him with eager interest.

"It's something new to be in danger, and rather exciting, don't you think?" said Beth. "But perhaps we're as safe as we would be at home."

"Once," said Louise, slowly, "there was a great eruption of Vesuvius which destroyed the cities of Herculaneum and Pompeii. Many of the inhabitants were buried alive. Perhaps they thought there was no real danger."

Uncle John scratched his head reflectively.

"I take it," he observed, "that the moral of your story is to light out while we have the chance."

"Not necessarily," observed the girl, smiling at his perplexity. "It is likewise true that many other eruptions have occurred, when little damage was done."

"Forewarned is forearmed," declared Patsy. "Naples isn't buried more than six inches in ashes, as yet, and it will take days for them to reach to our windows, provided they're falling at the same rate they do now. I don't see any use of getting scared before to-morrow, anyhow."

"It's a big hill," said Uncle John, gravely, "and I've no right to take foolish chances with three girls on my hands."

"I'm not frightened, Uncle John."

"Nor I."

"Nor I, the least bit."

"Everyone has left the hotel but ourselves," said he.

"How sorry they will be, afterward," remarked Beth.

He looked at them admiringly, and kissed each one.

"You stay in this room and don't move a peg till I get back," he enjoined them; "I'm going out to look over the situation."

CHAPTER VII
A FRIEND IN NEED

Some of Mr. Merrick's business friends in New York, hearing of his proposed trip, had given him letters of introduction to people in various European cities. He had accepted them--quite a bunch, altogether--but had firmly resolved not to use them. Neither he nor the nieces cared to make superficial acquaintances during their wanderings. Yet Uncle John chanced to remember that one of these letters was to a certain Colonel Angeli of the Twelfth Italian Regiment, occupying the barracks on the Pizzofalcone hill at Naples. This introduction, tendered by a relative of the Colonel's American wife, was now reposing in Mr. Merrick's pocket, and he promptly decided to make use of it in order to obtain expert advice as to the wisdom of remaining in the stricken city.

Enquiring his way from the still dazed concierge, he found that the Pizzofalcone barracks were just behind the hotel but several hundred feet above it; so he turned up the Strada St. Lucia and soon came upon the narrow lane that wound upward to the fortifications. It was a long and tedious climb in the semi-darkness caused by the steady fall of ashes, and at intervals the detonations from Vesuvius shook the huge rock and made its massive bulk seem insecure. But the little man persevered, and finally with sweating brow arrived at the barracks.

A soldier carried in the letter to his colonel and presently returned to usher Uncle John through the vast building, up a flight of steps, and so to a large covered balcony suspended many hundred feet above the Via Partenope, where the hotel was situated.

Here was seated a group of officers, watching intently the cloud that marked the location of the volcano. Colonel Angeli, big and bluff, his uniform gorgeous, his dark, heavy moustaches carefully waxed, his handsome face as ingenuous and merry as a schoolboy's, greeted the American with a gracious courtesy that made Uncle John feel quite at his ease. When he heard of the nieces the Italian made a grimace and then laughed.

"I am despairing, signore," said he, in English sufficiently strangulated to be amusing but nevertheless quite comprehensible, "that you and the sweet signorini are to see our lovely Naples under tribulations so very great. But yesterday, in all the world is no city so enchanting, so brilliant, so gay. To-day--look! is it not horrible? Vesuvio is sick, and Naples mourns until the tyrant is well again."

"But the danger," said Uncle John. "What do you think of the wisdom of our staying here? Is it safe to keep my girls in Naples during this eruption?"

"Ah! Why not? This very morning the mountain asunder burst, and we who love our people dread the news of devastation we shall hear. From the observatory, where His Majesty's faithful servant still remains, come telegrams that the great pebbles--what we call scoria--have ruined Ottajano and San Guiseppe. Perhaps they are overwhelmed. But the beast has vomited; he will feel better now, and ever become more quiet."

"I suppose," remarked Mr. Merrick, thoughtfully, "that no one knows exactly what the blamed hill may do next. I don't like to take chances with three girls on my hands. They are a valuable lot, Colonel, and worth saving."

The boyish Italian instantly looked grave. Then he led Uncle John away from the others, although doubtless he was the only officer present able to speak or understand English, and said to him:

"Where are you living?"

"At the hotel named after your sick mountain--the Vesuve."

"Very good. In the bay, not distant from your hotel, lies a government launch that is under my command. At my home in the Viala Elena are a wife and two children, who, should danger that is serious arise, will be put by my soldiers on the launch, to carry them to safety. Admirable, is it not?"

"Very good arrangement," said Uncle John.

"It renders me content to know that in any difficulty they cannot be hurt. I am not scare, myself, but it is pleasant to know I have what you call the side that is safe. From my American wife I have many of your excellent speech figures. But now! The launch is big. Remain happy in Naples--happy as Vesuvio will let you--and watch his vast, his gigantic exhibition. If danger come, you all enter my launch and be saved. If no danger, you have a marvelous experience." The serious look glided from his face, and was replaced by a smile as bright as before.

"Thank you very much," responded Uncle John, gratefully. "I shall go back to the girls well satisfied."

"Make the signorini stay in to-day," warned the colonel. "It is bad, just now, and so black one can nothing at all observe. To-morrow it will be better, and all can go without. I will see you myself, then, and tell you what to do."

Then he insisted that Uncle John clear his parched throat with a glass of vermouth--a harmless drink of which all Italians are very fond--and sent him away much refreshed in body and mind.

He made his way through the ashy rain back to the hotel. People were holding umbrellas over their heads and plodding through the dust with seeming unconcern. At one corner a street singer was warbling, stopping frequently to cough the lava dust from his throat or shake it from his beloved mandolin. A procession of peasants passed, chanting slowly and solemnly a religious hymn. At the head of the column was borne aloft a gilded statuette of the Virgin, and although Uncle John did not know it, these simple folks were trusting in the sacred image to avert further disaster from the angry mountain.

On arriving home Mr. Merrick told the girls with great elation of his new friend, and how they were to be taken aboard the launch in case of emergency.

"But how will we know when danger threatens?" asked Louise.

While Uncle John tried to think of an answer to this puzzling query someone knocked upon the door. The concierge was standing in the passage and beside him was a soldier in uniform, a natty cock's plume upon his beaver hat and a short carbine over his arm.

"A guard from Colonel Angeli, Signor," said the concierge, respectfully-- the first respectful tone he had yet employed.

The soldier took off his hat with a flourish, and bowed low.

"He is to remain in the hotel, sir, yet will not disturb you in any way," continued the whiskered one. "But should he approach you at any time and beckon you to follow him, do so at once, and without hesitation. It is Colonel Angeli's wish. You are in the charge of this brave man, who will watch over your welfare."

"That settles it, my dears," said Uncle John, cheerfully, when the soldier and the concierge had withdrawn. "This Italian friend doesn't do things by halves, and I take it we are perfectly safe from this time on."

CHAPTER VIII
ACROSS THE BAY

Tom Horton called an hour later. He was in despair because his party had decided to leave Naples for Rome, and he feared Beth would be engulfed by the volcano unless he was present to protect her.

"Mr. Merrick," said the boy, earnestly, "you'll take good care of Miss De Graf, sir, won't you? We both live in Ohio, you know, and we've just got acquainted; and--and I'd like to see her again, some time, if she escapes."

Uncle John's eyes twinkled, but he drew a long face.

"My dear Tom," he said, "don't ask me to take care of anyone--please don't! I brought these girls along to take care of me--three of 'em, sir--and they've got to do their duty. Don't you worry about the girls; just you worry about me."

That was not much consolation for the poor fellow, but he could do nothing more than wring their hands--Beth's twice, by mistake--and wish them good luck before he hurried away to rejoin his family.

"I'm sorry to see him go," said Beth, honestly. "Tom is a nice boy."

"Quite right," agreed Uncle John. "I hope we shall meet no worse fellows than Tom Horton."

At noon they were served a modest luncheon in their rooms, for Signor Floriano, having sent his important papers to a place of safety, had resolved to stick to his hotel and do his duty by any guests that chose to remain with him in defiance of the existent conditions. He had succeeded in retaining a few servants who had more courage than those that had stampeded at the first alarm, and while the hotel service for the next few days was very inadequate, no one was liable to suffer any great privation.

During the afternoon the gloom grew denser than before, while thicker than ever fell the rain of ashes. This was the worst day Naples experienced during the great eruption, and Uncle John and his nieces were content to keep their rooms and live in the glare of electric lights. Owing to their wise precautions to keep out the heavily laden air they breathed as little lava dust into their lungs as any people, perhaps, in the city; but to escape all was impossible. Their eyes and throats became more or less inflamed by the floating atoms, and the girls declared they felt as if they were sealed up in a tomb.

"Well, my chickens, how do you like being abroad, and actually in Europe?" enquired Uncle John, cheerfully.

Beth and Patsy smiled at him, but Louise looked up from the Baedecker she was studying and replied:

"It's simply delightful, Uncle, and I'm glad we happened here during this splendid eruption of Vesuvius. Only--only--"

"Only what, my dear?"

"Only it is such hard work to keep clean," answered his dainty niece. "Even the water is full of lava, and I'm sure my face looks like a chimney-sweep's."

"And you, Beth?"

"I don't like it, Uncle. I'm sure I'd prefer Naples in sunshine, although this is an experience we can brag about when we get home."

"That is the idea, exactly," said Louise, "and the only thing that reconciles me to the discomforts. Thousands see Naples in sunshine, but few can boast seeing Vesuvius in eruption. It will give us considerable prestige when we return home."

"Ah, that is why I selected this time to bring you here," declared Uncle John, with a comical wink. "I ordered the eruption before I left home, and I must say they've been very prompt about it, and done the thing up brown. Eh, Patsy?"

"Right you are, Uncle. But you might tell 'em to turn off the eruption now, because we've had enough."

"Don't like Eu-rope, eh?"

"Why, if I thought all Europe was surrounded by volcanoes, I'd go home at once, if I had to walk. But the geographies don't mention many of these spouters, so we may as well stick out our present experience and hope the rest of the continent will behave better. The Major'll be worried to death when he hears of this."

"I've sent him a cable," said Uncle John.

"What did you say?" asked Patsy, eagerly.

"'All safe and well and enjoying the fireworks.'"

"I'm glad you did that," replied the girl, deeply grateful at this evidence of thoughtfulness. "It's bad enough for the Major to have me away, without making him worry, into the bargain."

"Well, no one is likely to worry about me," said Beth, philosophically.

"Mother seldom reads the papers, except to get the society news," remarked Louise. "I doubt if she'll hear of the eruption, unless the Major happens to tell her."

"I've cabled them all," said Uncle John. "They're entitled to know that their kidiwinkles are in good shape."

The evening was a tedious one, although they tried to enliven it with a game of bridge, in which Uncle John and Louise were quite proficient and the others dreadfully incompetent. Once in a while the volcano thundered a deep detonation that caused the windows to shiver, but the Americans were getting used to the sound and paid little heed to it.

In the morning the wind had shifted, and although the air was still full of dust all near-by objects were clearly visible and even the outline of Vesuvius could be seen sending skyward its pillar of black smoke.

Colonel Angeli appeared soon after breakfast, his uniform fresh and bright and his boyish face beaming as pleasantly as ever.

"Vesuvio is better," said he, "but the rascal has badly acted and done much harm to our poor people. Like Herculaneum, our Boscatrecase is covered with lava; like Pompeii our Ottajano is buried in ashes. Let me advise you. To-day go to Sorrento, and there stay for a time, until we can the dust brush from our streets and prepare to welcome you with the comfort more serene. I must myself ride to the villages that are suffering. My men are already gone, with the Red-Cross corps, to succor whom they can. I will send to you word when you may return. Just now, should you stay, you will be able to see nothing at all."

"I believe that is wise counsel," replied Uncle John.

"Sorrento has no ashes," continued the Colonel, "and from there you may watch the volcano better than from Naples. To-day come the Duke and Duchess d'Aosta to render assistance to the homeless and hungry; to-morrow His Majesty the King will be here to discover what damage has been caused.

Alas! we have no sackcloth, but we are in ashes. I trust you will pardon my poor Naples for her present inhospitality."

"Sure thing," said Uncle John. "The city may be under a cloud, but her people are the right stuff, and we are greatly obliged to you for all your kindness to us."

"But that is so little!" said the colonel, deprecatingly.

They decided to leave their heavy baggage at the Hotel du Vesuve, and carried only their suit-cases and light luggage aboard the little steamer that was bound across the bay for Sorrento. The decks were thronged with people as eager to get away from the stricken city as were our friends, and Uncle John was only enabled to secure seats for his girls by bribing a steward so heavily that even that modern brigand was amazed at his good fortune.

The ride was short but very interesting, for they passed under the shadow of the smoking mountain and came into a fresh, sweet atmosphere that was guiltless of a speck of the disagreeable lava dust that had so long annoyed them. The high bluffs of Sorrento, with their picturesque villas and big hotels, seemed traced in burnished silver by the strong sunshine, and every member of Uncle John's party was glad that Colonel Angeli had suggested this pleasant change of condition.

Small boats took them ashore and an elevator carried them swiftly to the top of the cliff and deposited them on the terrace of the Victoria, a beautiful inn that nestled in a garden brilliant with splendid flowers and shrubbery. Here they speedily established themselves, preparing to enjoy their first real experience of "Sunny Italy."

CHAPTER IX
COUNT FERRALTI

At dinner it was announced that the famous Tarantella would be danced in the lower hall of the hotel at nine o'clock, and the girls told Uncle John that they must not miss this famous sight, which is one of the most unique in Sorrento, or indeed in all Italy.

As they entered the pretty, circular hall devoted to the dance Louise gave a start of surprise. A goodly audience had already assembled in the room, and among them the girl seemed to recognize an acquaintance, for after a brief hesitation she advanced and placed her hand in that of a gentleman who had risen on her entrance and hastened toward her.

He was a nice looking young fellow, Beth thought, and had a foreign and quite distinguished air.

Presently Louise turned with cheeks somewhat flushed and brought the gentleman to her party, introducing him to Uncle John and her cousins as Count Ferralti, whom she had once met in New York while he was on a visit to America.

The Count twirled his small and slender moustaches in a way that Patsy thought affected, and said in excellent English:

"It delights me to meet Mr. Merrick and the young ladies. May I express a hope that you are pleased with my beautiful country?"

"Are you Italian?" asked Uncle John, regarding the young man critically.

"Surely, Mr. Merrick. But I have resided much in New York, and may well claim to be an adopted son of your great city."

"New York adopts a good many," said Uncle John, drily. "It has even been thoughtless enough to adopt me."

The dancers entered at that moment and the Americans were forced to seat themselves hastily so as not to obstruct the view of others. Count Ferralti found a place beside Louise, but seemed to have little to say to her during the course of the entertainment.

The dances were unique and graceful, being executed by a troup of laughing peasants dressed in native costume, who seemed very proud of their accomplishment and anxious to please the throng of tourists present. The Tarantella originated in Ischia, but Sorrento and Capri have the best dancers.

Afterward Uncle John and his nieces stood upon the terrace and watched the volcano rolling its dense clouds, mingled with sparks of red-hot scoria, toward the sky. The Count clung to Louise's side, but also tried to make himself agreeable to her cousins. In their rooms that night Patsy told Beth that the young foreigner was "too highfalutin' to suit her," and Beth replied that his manners were so like those of their Cousin Louise that the two ought to get along nicely together.

Uncle John liked his nieces to make friends, and encouraged young men generally to meet them; but there was something in the appearance of this callow Italian nobleman that stamped his character as artificial and insincere. He resolved to find out something about his antecedents before he permitted the young fellow to establish friendly relations with his girls.

Next morning after breakfast he wandered through the lobby and paused at the little office, where he discovered that the proprietor of this hotel was a brother of that Floriano who managed the Hotel du Vesuve. That gave him an excuse to talk with the man, who spoke very good English and was exceedingly courteous to his guests--especially when they were American.

"I see you have Count Ferralti with you," remarked Uncle John.

"Whom, sir?"

"Ferralti--Count Ferralti. The young man standing by the window, yonder."

"I--I did not know," he said, hesitatingly. "The gentleman arrived last evening, and I had not yet learned his name. Let me see," he turned to his list of guests, who register by card and not in a book, and continued: "Ah, yes; he has given his name as Ferralti, but added no title. A count, did you say?"

"Yes," replied Uncle John.

The proprietor looked curiously toward the young man, whose back only was visible. Then he remarked that the eruption of Vesuvius was waning and the trouble nearly over for this time.

"Are the Ferraltis a good family?" asked Uncle John, abruptly.

"That I cannot tell you, Signor Merrick."

"Oh. Perhaps you know little about the nobility of your country."

"I! I know little of the nobility!" answered Floriano, indignantly. "My dear signor, there is no man better posted as to our nobility in all Italy."

"Yet you say you don't know the Ferralti family."

The proprietor reached for a book that lay above his desk.

"Observe, signor. Here is our record of nobility. It is the same as the 'Blue Book' or the 'Peerage' of England. Either fortunately or unfortunately--I cannot say--you have no need of such a book in America."

He turned the pages and ran his finger down the line of "Fs."

"Find me, if you can, a Count Ferralti in the list."

Uncle John looked. He put on his glasses and looked again. The name of Ferralti was no place in the record.

"Then there is no such count, Signor Floriano."

"And no such noble family, Signor Merrick."

Uncle John whistled softly and walked away to the window. The young man greeted him with a smile and a bow.

"I misunderstood your name last evening," he said. "I thought you were Count Ferralti."

"And that is right, sir," was the prompt reply. "Allow me to offer you my card."

Uncle John took the card and read:

"CONTE LEONARDI FERRALTI, Milano, Italia."

He carefully placed the card in his pocket-book.

"Thank you," said he. "It's a fine morning, Count."

"Charming, Mr. Merrick."

Uncle John walked away. He was glad that he had not suspected the young man unjustly. When an imposture is unmasked it is no longer dangerous.

He joined his nieces, who were all busily engaged in writing letters home, and remarked, casually:

"You've been deceived in your Italian friend, Louise. He is neither a count nor of noble family, although I suppose when you met him in New York he had an object in posing as a titled aristocrat."

The girl paused, examining the point of her pen thoughtfully.

"Are you sure, Uncle John?"

"Quite sure, my dear. I've just been through the list of Italian counts, and his name is not there. Floriano, the proprietor, who knows every aristocrat in Italy, has never before heard of him."

"How singular!" exclaimed Louise. "I wonder why he has tried to deceive us."

"Oh, the world is full of impostors; but when you are on to their game they are quite harmless. Of course we won't encourage this young man in any way. It will be better to avoid him."

"He--he seems very nice and gentlemanly," said Louise with hesitation.

The other girls exchanged glances, but made no remark. Uncle John hardly knew what to say further. He felt he was in an awkward position, for Louise was the most experienced in worldly ways of his three nieces and he had no desire to pose as a stern guardian or to deprive his girls of any passing pleasure they might enjoy. Moreover, Louise being in love with that young Weldon her mother so strongly objected to, she would not be likely to care much for this Italian fellow, and Mrs. Merrick had enjoined him to keep her daughter's mind from dwelling on her "entanglement."

"Oh, well, my dear," he said to her, "you must act as you see fit. I do not imagine we shall see much of this young man, in any event, and now that you are well aware of the fact that he is sailing under false colors, you will know how to handle him better than I can advise you."

"I shall be very careful," said Louise slowly, as she resumed her writing.

"Well then, girls, what do you say to a stroll around the village?" asked their uncle. "I'm told it's a proper place to buy silk stockings and inlaid wood-work. They come assorted, I suppose."

Beth and Patsy jumped up with alacrity, but Louise pleaded that she had several more letters to write; so the others left her and passed the rest of the forenoon in rummaging among the quaint shops of Sorrento, staring at the statue of Tasso, and enjoying the street scenes so vividly opposed to those of America. It was almost their first glimpse of foreign manners and customs. In Naples they had as yet seen nothing but darkness and falling ashes.

CHAPTER X
THE ROAD TO AMALFI

The Hotel Victoria faces the bay of Naples. Back of it are the famous gardens, and as you emerge from these you find yourself upon the narrow main street of Sorrento, not far from the Square of Tasso.

As our little party entered this street they were immediately espied by the vetturini, or cabmen, who rushed toward them with loud cries while they waved their whips frantically to attract attention. One tall fellow was dressed in a most imposing uniform of blue and gold, with a high hat bearing a cockade a la Inglese and shiny top boots. His long legs enabled him to outstrip the others, and in an almost breathless voice he begged Uncle John to choose his carriage: "the besta carrozza ina town!"

"We don't want to ride," was the answer.

The cabman implored. Certainly they must make the Amalfi drive, or to Massa Lubrense or Saint' Agata or at least Il Deserto! The others stood by to listen silently to the discussion, yielding first place to the victor in the race.

Uncle John was obdurate.

"All we want to-day is to see the town," he declared, "We're not going to ride, but walk."

"Ah, but the Amalfi road, signore! Surely you will see that."

"To-morrow, perhaps; not now."

"To-morrow, signore! It is good. At what hour, to-morrow, illustrissimo?"

"Oh, don't bother me."

"We may as well drive to Amalfi to-morrow," suggested Beth. "It is the proper thing to do, Uncle."

"All right; we'll go, then."

"You take my carrozza, signore?" begged the cabman. "It is besta ina town."

"Let us see it."

Instantly the crowd scampered back to the square, followed more leisurely by Uncle John and the girls. There the uniformed vetturio stood beside the one modern carriage in the group. It was new; it was glossy; it had beautiful, carefully brushed cushions; it was drawn by a pair of splendid looking horses.

"Is not bellissima, signore?" asked the man, proudly.

"All right," announced Uncle John, nodding approval. "Be ready to start at nine o'clock to-morrow morning."

The man promised, whereat his confreres lost all interest in the matter and the strangers were allowed to proceed without further interruption.

They found out all about the Amalfi drive that evening, and were glad indeed they had decided to go. Even Louise was pleased at the arrangement and as eager as the others to make the trip. It is one of the most famous drives in the world, along a road built upon the rocky cliff that overhangs the sea and continually winds in and out as it follows the outlines of the crags.

They had an early breakfast and were ready at nine o'clock; but when they came to the gate of the garden they found only a dilapidated carriage standing before it.

"Do you know where my rig is?" Uncle John asked the driver, at the same time peering up and down the road.

"It is me, sir signore. I am engage by you. Is it not so?"

Mr. Merrick looked at the driver carefully. It was long-legs, sure enough, but shorn of his beautiful regalia.

"Where's your uniform?" he asked.

"Ah, I have leave it home. The road is dusty, very; I must not ruin a nice dress when I work," answered the man, smiling unabashed.

"But the carriage. What has become of the fine carriage and the good horses, sir?"

"Ah, it is dreadful; it is horrible, signore. I find me the carrozza is not easy; it is not perfect; it do not remain good for a long ride. So I leave him home, for I am kind. I do not wish the signorini bella to tire and weep. But see the fine vetture you now have! Is he not easy like feathers, an' strong, an' molto buena?"

"It may be a bird, but it don't look it," said Uncle John, doubtfully. "I rented the best looking rig in town, and you bring me the worst."

"Only try, signore! Others may look; it is only you who must ride. You will be much please when we return."

"Well, I suppose we may as well take it," said the little man, in a resigned tone. "Hop in, my dears."

They entered the crazy looking vehicle and found the seats ample and comfortable despite the appearance of dilapidation everywhere prevalent. The driver mounted the box, cracked his whip, and the lean nags ambled away at a fair pace.

They passed near to the square, where the first thing that attracted Uncle John's attention was the beautiful turnout he had hired yesterday. It was standing just as it had before, and beside it was another man dressed in the splendid uniform his driver had claimed that he had left at home.

"Here--stop! Stop, I say!" he yelled at the man, angrily. But the fellow seemed suddenly deaf, and paid no heed. He cracked his whip and rattled away through the streets without a glance behind him. The girls laughed and Uncle John stopped waving his arms and settled into his seat with a groan.

"We've been swindled, my dears," he said; "swindled most beautifully. But I suppose we may as well make the best of it."

"Better," agreed Patsy. "This rig is all right, Uncle. It may not be as pretty as the other, but I expect that one is only kept to make engagements with. When it comes to actual use, we don't get it."

"That's true enough," he returned. "But I'll get even with this rascal before I've done with him, never fear."

It was a cold, raw morning, but the portiere at the Victoria had told them the sun would be out presently and the day become more genial. Indeed, the sun did come out, but only to give a discouraged look at the landscape and retire again. During this one day in which they rode to Amalfi and back, Uncle John afterward declared that they experienced seven different kinds of weather. They had sunshine, rain, hail, snow and a tornado; and then rain again and more sunshine. "Sunny Italy" seemed a misnomer that day, as indeed it does many days in winter and spring, when the climate is little better than that prevailing in the eastern and central portions of the United States. And perhaps one suffers more in Italy than in America, owing to the general lack of means to keep warm on cold days. The Italian, shivering and blue, will tell you it is not cold at all, for he will permit no reproach to lie on his beloved land; but the traveller frequently becomes discouraged, and the American contingent, especially, blames those misleading English writers who, finding relief from their own bleak island in Italian climes, exaggerated the conditions by apostrophizing the country as "Sunny Italy" and for more than a century uttered such rhapsodies in its praise that the whole world credited them--until it acquired personal experience of the matter.

Italy is beautiful; it is charming and delightful; but seldom is this true in winter or early spring.

The horses went along at a spanking pace that was astonishing. They passed through the picturesque lanes of Sorrento, climbed the further slope, and brought the carriage to the other side of the peninsula, where the girls obtained their first view of the Gulf of Salerno, with the lovely Isles of the Sirens lying just beneath them.

And now they were on the great road that skirts the coast as far as Salerno, and has no duplicate in all the known world. For it is cut from the solid rock of precipitous cliffs rising straight from the sea, which the highway overhangs at an average height of five hundred feet, the traveller being protected only by a low stone parapet from the vast gulf that yawns beneath. And on the other side of the road the cliffs continue to ascend a like distance toward the sky, their irregular surfaces dotted with wonderful houses that cling to the slopes, and vineyards that look as though they might slip down at any moment upon the heads of timorous pilgrims.

When it rained they put up the carriage top, which afforded but partial shelter. The shower was brief, but was shortly followed by hail as big as peas, which threatened to dash in the frail roof of their carrozza. While they shrank huddled beneath the blankets, the sun came out suddenly, and the driver shed his leathern apron, cracked his whip, and began singing merrily as the vehicle rolled over the smooth road.

Our travellers breathed again, and prepared to enjoy once more the wonderful vistas that were unfolded at every turn of the winding way. Sometimes they skirted a little cove where, hundreds of feet below, the fishermen sat before their tiny huts busily mending their nets. From that distance the boats drawn upon the sheltered beach seemed like mere toys. Then they would span a chasm on a narrow stone bridge, or plunge through an arch dividing the solid mountain. But ever the road returned in a brief space to the edge of the sea-cliff, and everywhere it was solid as the hills themselves, and seemingly as secure.

They had just sighted the ancient town of Positano and were circling a gigantic point of rock, when the great adventure of the day overtook them.

Without warning the wind came whistling around them in a great gale, which speedily increased in fury until it drove the blinded horses reeling against the low parapet and pushed upon the carriage as if determined to dash it over the precipice.

As it collided against the stone wall the vehicle tipped dangerously, hurling the driver from his seat to dive headforemost into the space beneath. But the man clung to the reins desperately, and they arrested his fall, leaving him dangling at the end of them while the maddened horses, jerked at the bits by the weight of the man, reared and plunged as if they would in any instant tumble themselves and the carriage over the cliff.

At this critical moment a mounted horseman, who unobserved had been following the party, dashed to their rescue. The rider caught the plunging steeds by their heads and tried to restrain their terror, at his own eminent peril, while the carriage lay wedged against the wall and the driver screamed pitifully from his dangerous position midway between sea and sky.

Then Beth slipped from her seat to the flat top of the parapet, stepped boldly to where the reins were pulling upon the terrified horses, and seized them in her strong grasp.

"Hold fast," she called calmly to the driver, and began dragging him upward, inch by inch.

He understood instantly the task she had undertaken, and in a moment his courage returned and he managed to get his foot in a crack of the rock and assist her by relieving her of part of his weight. Just above was a slight ledge; he could reach it now; and then she had him by the arm, so that another instant found him clinging to the parapet and drawing himself into a position of safety.

The wind had died away as suddenly as it came upon them. The horses, as soon as the strain upon their bits was relaxed, were easily quieted. Before those in the carriage had quite realized what had occurred the adventure was accomplished, the peril was past, and all was well again.

Uncle John leaped from the carriage, followed by Louise and Patsy. The young horseman who had come to their assistance so opportunely was none other than Count Ferralti, whom they had such good reason to distrust. He was sitting upon his horse and staring with amazement at Beth, at whose feet the driver was grovelling while tears flowed down his bronzed cheeks and he protested in an absurd mixture of English and Italian, by every saint in the calendar, that the girl had saved him from a frightful death and he would devote his future life to her service.

"It is wonderful!" murmured Ferralti. "However could such a slip of a girl do so great a deed?"

"Why, it's nothing at all," returned Beth, flushing; "we're trained to do such things in the gymnasium at Cloverton, and I'm much stronger than I appear to be."

"'Twas her head, mostly," said Patsy, giving her cousin an admiring hug; "she kept her wits while the rest of us were scared to death."

Uncle John had been observing the Count. One of the young man's hands hung limp and helpless.

"Are you hurt, sir?" he asked.

Ferralti smiled, and his eyes rested upon Louise.

"A little, perhaps, Mr. Merrick; but it is unimportant. The horses were frantic at the time and wrenched my wrist viciously as I tried to hold them. I felt something snap; a small bone, perhaps. But I am sure it is nothing of moment."

"We'd better get back to Sorrento," said Uncle John, abruptly.

"Not on my account, I beg of you," returned Ferralti, quickly. "We are half way to Amalfi now, and you may as well go on. For my part, if the wrist troubles me, I will see a surgeon at Amalfi--that is, if you permit me to accompany you."

He said this with a defferent bow and a glance of inquiry.

Uncle John could not well refuse. The young fellow might be a sham count, but the manliness and courage he had displayed in their grave emergency surely entitled him to their grateful consideration.

"You are quite welcome to join us," said Uncle John.

The driver had by now repaired a broken strap and found his equippage otherwise uninjured.

The horses stood meekly quiescent, as if they had never known a moment's fear in their lives. So the girls and their uncle climbed into the vehicle again and the driver mounted the box and cracked his whip with his usual vigor.

The wind had subsided as suddenly as it had arisen, and as they passed through Positano--which is four hundred feet high, the houses all up and down the side of a cliff like swallows' nests--big flakes of snow were gently falling around them.

Count Ferralti rode at the side of the carriage but did not attempt much conversation. His lips were tight set and the girls, slyly observing his face, were sure his wrist was hurting him much more than he cared to acknowledge.

Circling around the cliff beyond Positano the sun greeted them, shining from out a blue sky, and they wondered what had become of the bad weather they had so lately experienced.

From now on, past Prajano and into Amalfi, the day was brilliant and the temperature delightful. It was full noon by the time they alighted at the little gate-house of the ancient Cappuccini-Convento, now a hotel much favored by the tourist. Count Ferralti promised to join them later and rode on to the town to find a surgeon to look after his injured hand, while the others slowly mounted the long inclines leading in a zigzag fashion up to the old monastery, which was founded in the year 1212.

From the arbored veranda of this charming retreat is obtained one of the finest views in Europe, and while the girls sat enjoying it Uncle John arranged with a pleasant faced woman (who had once lived in America) for their luncheon.

An hour later, and just as they were sitting down to the meal, Count Ferralti rejoined them. His hand was bandaged and supported by a sling, and in answer to Louise's gentle inquiries he said, simply:

"It was as I had feared: a small bone snapped. But my surgeon is skillful, and says time will mend the wrist as good as new."

In spite of his courage he could eat no luncheon, but merely sipped a glass of wine; so Uncle John, alarmed at his pallor, insisted that he take a seat in the carriage on the return journey. Beth wanted to ride the Count's horse home, but there was no side saddle to be had, so they led the animal by a halter fastened behind the ricketty carriage, and Beth mounted the box and rode beside her friend the driver.

The pleasant weather lasted until they neared Sorrento, when another shower of rain came up. They reached their hotel damp and bedraggled, but enthusiastic over their wonderful trip and the interesting adventure it had incidentally developed.

CHAPTER XI
THE EAGLE SCREAMS

Despite the glories of the Amalfi road our tourists decided it was more pleasant to loiter around Sorrento for a time than to undertake further excursions. The mornings and evenings were chill, but during the middle of the day the air was warm and delicious; so the girls carried their books and fancy-work into the beautiful gardens or wandered lazily through the high-walled lanes that shut in the villas and orange groves. Sometimes they found a gate open, and were welcomed to the orchards and permitted to pluck freely the fragrant and rich flavored fruit, which is excelled in no other section of the south country. Also Uncle John, with Beth and Patsy, frequented the shops of the wood-workers and watched their delicate and busy fingers inlaying the various colored woods; but Louise mostly kept to the garden, where Count Ferralti, being a semi-invalid, was content to sit by her side and amuse her.

In spite of her uncle's discovery of the false position assumed by this young man, Louise seemed to like his attentions and to approve his evident admiration for her. His ways might be affected and effeminate and his conversational powers indifferent; but his bandaged wrist was a constant reminder to all the nieces that he possessed courage and ready wit, and it was but natural that he became more interesting to them because just now he was to an extent helpless, and his crippled hand had been acquired in their service.

Uncle John watched the young fellow shrewdly, but could discover little harm in him except his attempt to deceive them in regard to his name and position. Yet in his mature eyes there was not much about Ferralti to arouse admiration, and the little man considered his girls too sensible to be greatly impressed by this youthful Italian's personality. So he allowed him to sit with his nieces in the gardens as much as he pleased, believing it would be ungrateful to deprive the count of that harmless recreation.

"A reg'lar chaperone might think differently," he reflected; "but thank goodness there are no dragons swimming in our cup of happiness."

One day they devoted to Capri and the Blue Grotto, and afterward they lunched at the Quisisana and passed the afternoon in the town. But the charms of Sorrento were too great for Capri to win their allegiance, and they were glad to get back to their quaint town and delightful gardens again.

The week passed all too swiftly, and then came a letter from Colonel Angeli telling them to return to Naples and witness the results of the eruption. This they decided to do, and bidding good-bye to Signor Floriano and his excellent hotel they steamed across the bay and found the "Vesuve" a vastly different hostelry from the dismal place they had left in their flight from Naples. It was now teeming with life, for, all danger being past, the tourists had flocked to the city in droves. The town was still covered with ashes, but under the brilliant sunshine it did not look as gloomy as one might imagine, and already thousands of carts were busily gathering the dust from the streets and dumping it in the waters of the bay. It would require months of hard work, though, before Naples could regain a semblance of its former beauty.

Their friend the Colonel personally accompanied them to the towns that had suffered the most from the eruption. At Boscatrecasa they walked over the great beds of lava that had demolished the town--banks of cinders looking like lumps of pumice stone and massed from twenty to thirty feet in thickness throughout the valley. The lava was still so hot that it was liable to blister the soles of their feet unless they kept constantly moving. It would be many more days before the interior of the mass became cold.

Through the forlorn, dust-covered vineyards they drove to San Guiseppe, where a church roof had fallen in and killed one hundred and forty people, maiming many more. The Red-Cross tents were pitched in the streets and the whole town was one vast hospital. Ottajano, a little nearer to the volcano, had been buried in scoria, and nine-tenths of the roofs had fallen in, rendering the dwellings untenable.

From here a clear view of Mt. Vesuvius could be obtained. The shape of the mountain had greatly altered and the cone had lost sixty-five feet of its altitude. But when one gazed upon the enormous bulk of volcanic deposit that littered the country for miles around, it seemed to equal a dozen mountains the size of Vesuvius. The marvel was that so much ashes and cinders could come from a single crater in so short a period.

Naples was cleaning house, but slowly and listlessly. The people seemed as cheerful and light-hearted as ever. The volcano was one of their crosses, and they bore it patiently. The theatres would remain closed for some weeks to come, but the great Museo Nationale was open, and Uncle John and his nieces were much interested in the bronze and marble statuary that here form the greatest single collection in all the world.

It was at the Museum that Mr. Merrick was arrested for the first time in his life, an experience he never afterward forgot.

Bad money is so common in Naples that Uncle John never accepted any change from anyone, but obtained all his silver coins and notes directly from the Banca Commerciale Italiana, a government institution. One morning he drove with the girls to the museum and paid the cabman a lira, but before he could ascend the steps the man was after him and holding out a leaden coin, claiming that his fare had given him bad money and must exchange it for good. This is so common a method of swindling that Uncle John paid no heed to the demands of the cabman until one of the Guard Municipale, in his uniform of dark blue with yellow buttons and cap, placed a restraining hand upon the American's shoulder.

Uncle John angrily shook him off, but the man persisted, and an interpreter employed by the museum stepped forward and explained that unless the cabman was given a good coin in exchange for the bad one the guarde would be obliged to take him before a commissionaire, or magistrate.

"But I gave him a good coin--a lira direct from the bank," declared Uncle John.

"He exhibits a bad one," returned the interpreter, calmly.

"He's a swindler!"

"He is a citizen of Naples, and entitled to a just payment," said the other, shrugging his shoulders.

"You are all leagued together," said Uncle John, indignantly. "But you will get no more money out of me, I promise you."

The result was that the stubborn American was placed under arrest. Leaving the girls at the museum in charge of Ferralti, who had made no attempt to interfere in the dispute but implored Uncle John to pay and avoid trouble, the angry prisoner was placed in the same cab he had arrived in and, with the officer seated beside him, was publicly driven to the office of the magistrate.

This official understood no English, but he glowered and frowned fiercely when the American was brought before him. The guarde and the cabman stood with bared bowed heads and in low tones preferred the charge against the prisoner; but Uncle John swaggered up to the desk and pounded his clinched fist upon it while he roared a defiance of Italian injustice and threatened to "bring over a few war-ships and blow Naples into kingdom come!"

The magistrate was startled, and ordered the prisoner searched for concealed weapons. Uncle John doubled his fists and dared the guarde to touch him.

Then the cabman was dispatched for someone who could speak English, and when an interpreter arrived the American told him to send for the United States consul and also to inform the magistrate that nothing but war between America and Italy could wipe out the affront that had been thrust upon him.

The magistrate was disturbed, and preferred not to send for the consul. He offered to release Uncle John if he would give the cabman a good lira in exchange for the bad one. The official fee would be five lira--or say three lira--or even two. Uncle John flatly refused to pay anything to anybody. Only war could settle this international complication--bloody and bitter war. The consul must cable at once for war-ships and troops. He would insist upon it. All compromise was now impossible!

The magistrate was frightened. The guarde's eyes bulged with horror and he trembled visibly. It was evident they had made a grave mistake in arresting this mad American, who was evidently a personage of great importance and able to declare war at a moment's notice. The cabman, the magistrate, the guarde and the interpreter put their heads together and chattered voluble Italian--all speaking at once in excited tones--while Uncle John continued to warn them at the top of his lungs that their country was doomed to sudden annihilation and they were the culprits responsible for the coming calamity.

As a result they bundled the irate American into the carriage again and drove him poste haste back to the museum, where they deposited him upon the steps. Then in a flash the guarde and the cabman disappeared from sight and were seen no more.

The victor smiled proudly as his nieces rushed toward him.

"Did you have to pay another lira, Uncle?" asked Patsy, anxiously.

"Not on your life, my dear," mopping his brow vigorously. "They're a lot of cutthroats and assassins--policemen, magistrates and all--but when the eagle screams they're wise enough to duck."

The girls laughed.

"And did the eagle scream, then?" Patsy enquired.

"Just a little, my dear; but if it whispered it would sound mighty loud in this mummified old world. But we've lost enough time for one day. Come; let's go see 'Narcissus' and the 'Dancing Faun.'"

CHAPTER XII
MOVING ON

"Here's a letter from my dear old friend Silas Watson," said Uncle John, delightedly. "It's from Palermo, where he has been staying with his ward--and your friend, girls--Kenneth Forbes, and he wants me to lug you all over to Sicily at once."

"That's jolly," said Patsy, with a bright smile. "I'd like to see Kenneth again."

"I suppose he is a great artist, by this time," said Beth, musingly.

"How singular!" exclaimed Louise. "Count Ferralti told me only this morning that he had decided to go to Palermo."

"Really?" said Uncle John.

"Yes, Uncle. Isn't it a coincidence?"

"Why, as for that," he answered, slowly, "I'm afraid it will prevent our seeing the dear count--or whatever he is--again, at least for some time. For Mr. Watson and Kenneth are just leaving Palermo, and he asks us to meet him in another place altogether, a town called--called--let me see; Tormenti, or Terminal, or something."

"Give me the letter, dear," said Patsy. "I don't believe it's Terminal at all. Of course not," consulting the pages, "it's Taormina."

"Is that in Sicily?" he asked.

"Yes. Listen to what Mr. Watson says: 'I'm told it is the most beautiful spot in the world, which is the same thing you hear about most beautiful places. It is eight hundred feet above the Mediterranean and nestles peacefully in the shadow of Mount Etna.'"

"Etna!" cried Uncle John, with a start. "Isn't that another volcano?"

"To be sure," said Beth, the geographer. "Etna is the biggest volcano in the world."

"Does it spout?" he asked, anxiously.

Aunt Jane's Nieces Abroad | 63

"All the time, they say. But it is not usually dangerous."

"The proper thing, when you go to Eu-rope," declared Uncle John, positively, "is to do Venice, where the turpentine comes from, and Switzerland, where they make chocolate and goat's milk, and Paris and Monte Carlo, where they kick high and melt pearls in champagne. Everybody knows that. That's what goin' to Eu-rope really means. But Sicily isn't on the programme, that I ever heard of. So we'll just tell Silas Watson that we'll see him later-- which means when we get home again."

"But Sicily is beautiful," protested Patsy. "I'd as soon go there as anywhere."

"It's a very romantic place," added Louise, reflectively.

"Everybody goes to France and Switzerland," remarked Beth. "But it's because they don't know any better. Let's be original, Uncle, and keep out of the beaten track of travel."

"But the volcano!" exclaimed Mr. Merrick. "Is it necessary to stick to volcanoes to be original?"

"Etna won't hurt us, I'm sure," said Patsy.

"Isn't there a Greek theatre at Taormina?" asked Louise.

"I've never heard of it; but I suppose the Greeks have, if it's there," he replied. "But why not wait till we get home, and then go to Kieth's or Hammerstein's?"

"You don't understand, dear. This theatre is very ancient."

"Playing minstrel shows in it yet, I suppose. Well, girls, if you say Sicily, Sicily it is. All I'm after is to give you a good time, and if you get the volcano habit it isn't my fault."

"It is possible the Count said Taormina, instead of Palermo," remarked Louise, plaintively. "I wasn't paying much attention at the time. I'll ask him."

The others ignored this suggestion. Said Patsy to her uncle:

"When do we go, sir?"

"Whenever you like, my dears."

"Then I vote to move on at once," decided the girl. "We've got the best out of Naples, and it's pretty grimey here yet."

The other nieces agreed with her, so Uncle John went out to enquire the best way to get to Sicily, and to make their arrangements.

The steamer "Victor Emmanuel" of the Navigazione General Italiana line was due to leave Naples for Messina the next evening, arriving at its destination the following morning. Uncle John promptly booked places. The intervening day was spent in packing and preparing for the journey, and like all travellers the girls were full of eager excitement at the prospect of seeing something new.

"I'm told Sicily is an island," grumbled Uncle John. "Here we are, on a trip to Eu-rope, and emigrating to an island the first thing we do."

"Sicily is Europe, all right, Uncle," answered Patsy. "At least, it isn't Asia or Africa."

That assertion seemed to console him a little, and he grew cheerful again.

The evening was beautiful as they embarked, but soon after leaving the bay the little, tub-shaped steamer began to tumble and toss vigorously, so that all the passengers aboard speedily sought their berths.

Uncle John found himself in a stuffy little cabin that smelled of tar and various other flavors that were too mixed to be recognizable. As a result he passed one of the most miserable nights of his life.

Toward morning he rolled out and dressed himself, preferring the deck to his bed, and the first breath of salt air did much to restore him. Day was just breaking, and to the right he could see a tongue of fire flaming against the dark sky.

"What is that, sir?" he enquired of an officer who passed.

"That is Stromboli, signor, the great volcano of Lipari. It is always in eruption."

Uncle John groaned.

"Volcanoes to right of us, volcanoes to left of us volleyed and thundered," he muttered dismally, as he fell back in his chair.

The sky brightened, and the breath of the breeze changed and came to him laden with delicious fragrance.

"See, signore!" called the officer, passing again; "before us is mighty Etna--you can see it clearly from the bow."

"Volcanoes in front of us, volcanoes behind us!" wailed the little man. But he walked to the bow and saw the shores of Sicily looming in advance, with the outline of the stately mountain rising above and dominating it.

Then the sun burst forth, flooding all with a golden radiance that was magical in its gorgeous effects. Patsy came on deck and stood beside her uncle, lost in rapturous admiration. Beth soon followed her.

Before long they entered the Straits of Messina and passed between the classic rock of Scylla on the Calabrian coast, and the whirlpool of Charybdis at the point of the promontory of Faro, which forms the end of the famous "Golden Sickle" enclosing the Bay of Messina.

"If this is really Eu-rope, I'm glad we came," said Uncle John, drawing a long breath as the ship came to anchor opposite the Palazzo Municipale. "I don't remember seeing anything prettier since we left New York."

Presently they had loaded their trunks and hand baggage, and incidentally themselves, into the boat of the Hotel Trinacria which came alongside in charge of a sleepy porter. After a brief examination at the custom-house, where Uncle John denied having either sugar, tobacco or perfumery, they followed on foot the truck laden with their worldly possessions, and soon reached the hotel.

A pleasant breakfast followed, which they ate before a window overlooking the busy marina, and then they drove about the town for a time to see in a casual way the "sights." In the afternoon they took the train for Taormina. Messina seemed a delightful place, but if they were going to settle in Taormina for a time it would not pay them to unpack or linger on the way.

So they rolled along the coast for a couple of hours in a quaint, old-fashioned railway carriage, and were then deposited upon the platform of the little station at Giardini.

"I'm afraid there has been a mistake," said the little man, gazing around him anxiously. "There's no town here, and I told the guard to put us off at Taormina--not this forlorn place."

Just then Beth discovered a line of carriages drawn up back of the station. The drivers were mostly asleep inside them, although several stood in a group arguing in fluent Italian the grave question as to whether Signora Gani's cow had a black patch over its left shoulder, or not.

Some of the carriages bore signs: "Hotel Timeo;" "Grand Hotel San Domenico;" "Hotel Castello-a-Mare;" "Grand Hotel Metropole," and so forth. In that of the Castello-a-Mare the man was awakening and rubbing his eyes. Uncle John said to him:

"Good morning. Had a nice rest?"

"I thank you, signore, I am well refreshed," was the reply.

"By the way, can you tell us where the town of Taormina is? I hate to trouble you; but we'd like to know."

The man waved an arm upward, and following the motion with their eyes they saw a line of precipitous cliffs that seemed impossible to scale.

"Do you desire to go to the Grand Hotel Castello-a-Mare?" enquired the driver, politely.

"Is it in Taormina?"

"Most certainly, signore."

"And you will take us?"

"With pleasure, signore."

"Oh; I didn't know. I supposed you were going to sleep again."

The man looked at him reproachfully.

"It is my business, signore. I am very attentive to my duties. If you permit me to drive you to our splendide--our magnifico hotel--you will confer a favor."

"How about the baggage?"

"The trunks, signor, we will send for later. There is really no hurry about them. The small baggage will accompany us. You will remark how excellent is my English. I am Frascatti Vietri; perhaps you have heard of me in America?"

"If I have it has escaped my memory," said Uncle John, gravely.

"Have you been to America?" asked Beth.

"Surely, signorina. I lived in Chicago, which, as you are aware, is America. My uncle had a fruit shop in South Water, a via which is Chicago. Is it not so? You will find few in Taormina who can the English speak, and none at all who can so perfectly speak it as Frascatti Vietri."

"You are wonderful," said Patsy, delighted with him. But Uncle John grew impatient to be off.

"I hate to interrupt you, Mr. Vietri," he hinted; "but if you can spare the time we may as well make a start."

The driver consented. He gracefully swung the suit-cases and travelling bags to the top of the vehicle and held the door open while his fares entered. Then he mounted to his seat, took the reins, and spoke to the horses. Some of the other drivers nodded at him cheerfully, but more as if they were sorry he must exert himself than with any resentment at his success in getting the only tourists who had alighted from the train.

As they moved away Uncle John said: "Observe the difference between the cab-drivers here and those at home. In America they fight like beasts to get a job; here they seem anxious to avoid earning an honest penny. If there could be a happy medium somewhere, I'd like it."

"Are we going to the best hotel?" asked Louise, who had seemed a trifle disconsolate because she had not seen Count Ferralti since leaving Naples.

"I don't know, my dear. It wasn't a question of choice, but of necessity. No other hotel seemed willing to receive us."

They were now winding upward over a wonderful road cut in the solid rock. It was broad and smooth and protected by a parapet of dressed limestone. Now and then they passed pleasant villas set in orchards of golden oranges or groves of olives and almonds; but there was no sign of life on any side.

The road was zigzag, making a long ascent across the face of the cape, then turning abruptly to wind back again, but always creeping upward until an open space showed the station far below and a rambling stone building at the edge of the cliff far above.

"Behold!" cried Frascatti, pointing up, "the Grand Hotel Castello-a-Mare; is it not the excellenza location?"

"Has it a roof?" asked Uncle John, critically.

"Of a certainty, signore! But it does not show from below," was the grave reply.

At times Frascatti stopped his horses to allow them to rest, and then he would turn in his seat to address his passengers in the open victoria and descant upon the beauties of the panorama each turn unfolded.

"This road is new," said he, "because we are very progressive and the old road was most difficulty. Then it was three hours from the bottom to the top. Now it is but a short hour, for our energy climbs the three miles in that brief time. Shall I stop here for the sunset, or will your excellenzi hasten on?"

"If your energy approves, we will hasten," returned Uncle John. "We love a sunset, because it's bound to set anyway, and we may as well make the best of it; but we have likewise an objection to being out after dark. Any brigands around here?"

"Brigands! Ah; the signor is merry. Never, since the days of Naxos, have brigands infested our fair country."

"When were the days of Naxos?"

"Some centuries before Christ, signor," bowing his head and making the sign of the cross.

"Very good. The brigands of those days must, of course, be dead by this time. Now, sir, when you have leisure, let us hasten."

The horses started and crept slowly upward again. None of the party was in a hurry. Such beautiful glimpses of scenery were constantly visible from the bends of the road that the girls were enraptured, and could have ridden for hours in this glorious fairyland.

But suddenly the horses broke into a trot and dragged the carriage rapidly forward over the last incline. A moment later they dashed into the court of the hotel and the driver with a loud cry of "Oo-ah!" and a crack of his whip drew up before the entrance.

The portiere and the padrone, or landlord--the latter being also the proprietaire--came out to greet them, extending to their guests a courteous welcome. The house was very full. All of the cheaper rooms were taken; but of course the Signor Americain would wish only the best and be glad to pay.

Uncle John requested them to rob him as modestly as possible without conflicting with their sense of duty, and they assured him they would do so.

The rooms were adorable. They faced the sea and had little balconies that gave one a view of the blue Mediterranean far beneath, with lovely Isola Bella and the Capo San Andrea nestling on its bosom. To the right towered the majestic peak of Etna, its crest just now golden red in the dying sunset.

The girls drew in deep breaths and stood silent in a very ecstacy of delight. At their feet was a terraced garden, running downward two hundred feet to where the crag fell sheer to the sea. It was glorious with blooming flowers of every sort that grows, and the people on the balconies imagined at the moment they had been transferred to an earthly paradise too fair and sweet for ordinary mortals. And then the glow of the sun faded softly and twilight took its place. Far down the winding road could be seen the train of carriages returning from the station, the vetturini singing their native songs as the horses slowly ascended the slope. An unseen organ somewhere in the distance ground out a Neapolitan folk song, and fresh and youthful voices sang a clear, high toned accompaniment.

Even practical Uncle John stood absorbed and admiring until the soft voice of the facchino called to ask if he wanted hot water in which to bathe before dinner.

"It's no use," said Patsy, smiling at him from the next balcony with tears in her eyes; "There's not another Taormina on earth. Here we are, and here we stay until we have to go home again."

"But, my dear, think of Paris, of Venice, of--"

"I'll think of nothing but this, Uncle John. Unless you settle down with us here I'll turn milkmaid and live all my days in Sicily!"

Beth laughed, and drew her into their room.

"Don't be silly, Patsy dear," she said, calmly, although almost as greatly affected as her cousin. "There are no cows here, so you can't be a milkmaid."

"Can't I milk the goats, then?"

"Why, the men seem to do that, dear. But cheer up. We've only seen the romance of Taormina yet; doubtless it will be commonplace enough to-morrow."

CHAPTER XIII
IL DUCA

Beth's prediction, however, did not come true. The morning discovered nothing commonplace about Taormina. Their hotel was outside the walls, but a brief walk took them to the Messina Gate, a quaint archway through which they passed into the narrow streets of one of the oldest towns in Sicily. Doorways and windows of Saracen or Norman construction faced them on every side, and every inch of the ancient buildings was picturesque and charming.

Some of the houses had been turned into shops, mostly for the sale of curios. Uncle John and his nieces had scarcely passed a hundred yards into the town when one of these shops arrested their attention. It was full of antique jewelry, antique furniture, antique laces and antique pottery--all of the most fascinating description. The jewelry was tarnished and broken, the lace had holes in it and the furniture was decrepit and unsteady; but the proprietor cared nothing for such defects. All was very old, and he knew the tourist was eager to buy. So he scattered his wares inside and outside his salesroom, much as the spider spreads his web for the unwary, and waited for the inevitable tourist with a desire to acquire something ancient and useless.

The girls could not be induced to pass the shop. They entered the square, low room and flooded the shopman with eager questions. Notwithstanding Frascatti's assertion that few in Taormina could speak English, this man was quite intelligible and fixed his prices according to the impression his wares made upon the artistic sense of the young American ladies.

It was while they were intently inspecting some laces that the proprietor suddenly paused in his chatter, removed his hat and bowed almost to the floor, his face assuming at the same time a serious and most humble expression.

Turning around they saw standing outside the door a man whom they recognized at once as their fellow passenger aboard the "Princess Irene."

"Oh, Signor Valdi!" cried Patsy, running toward him, "how strange to find you again in this out-of-the-way place."

The Italian frowned, but in a dignified manner took the hand of all three girls in turn and then bowed a greeting to Mr. Merrick.

Uncle John thought the fellow had improved in appearance. Instead of the flannel shirt and Prince Albert coat he had affected on shipboard he now wore a native costume of faded velvet, while a cloak of thin but voluminous cloth swung from his shoulders, and a soft felt hat shaded his dark eyes.

His appearance was entirely in keeping with the place, and the American noticed that the villagers who passed doffed their hats most respectfully to this seemingly well-known individual. But mingled with their polite deference was a shyness half fearful, and none stopped to speak but hurried silently on.

"And how do we happen to find you here, Signor Valdi?" Patsy was saying. "Do you live in Taormina?"

"I am of this district, but not of Taormina," he replied. "It is chance that you see me here. Eh, Signor Bruggi, is it not so?" casting one of his characteristic fierce glances at the shopkeeper.

"It is so, your excellency."

"But I am glad you have come to the shadow of Etna," he continued, addressing the Americans with slow deliberation. "Here the grandeur of the world centers, and life keeps time with Nature. You will like it? You will stay?"

"Oh, for a time, anyway," said Patsy.

"We expect to meet some friends here," explained Uncle John. "They are coming down from Palermo, but must have been delayed somewhere on the way."

"Who are they?" asked Valdi, brusquely.

"Americans, of course; Silas Watson and Kenneth Forbes. Do you know of them?"

"No," said the other. He cast an uneasy glance up and down the street. "I will meet you again, signorini," he added. "Which is your hotel?"

"The Castello-a-Mare. It is delightful," said Beth.

He nodded, as if pleased. Then, folding his cloak about him, he murmured "adios!" and stalked away without another word or look.

"Queer fellow," remarked Uncle John.

The shopkeeper drew a long breath and seemed relieved.

"Il Duca is unusual, signore," he replied.

"Duke!" cried the girls, in one voice.

The man seemed startled.

"I--I thought you knew him; you seemed friends," he stammered.

"We met Signor Valdi on shipboard," said Uncle John.

"Valdi? Ah, yes; of course; the duke has been to America."

"Isn't his name Valdi?" asked Beth, looking the man straight in the eyes. "Has he another name here, where he lives?"

The shopman hesitated.

"Who knows?" was the evasive reply. "Il Duca has many names, but we do not speak them. When it is necessary to mention him we use his title--the duke."

"Why?" asked the girl.

"Why, signorina? Why? Perhaps because he does not like to be talked about. Yes; that is it, I am sure."

"Where does he live?" asked Patsy.

The man seemed uneasy under so much questioning.

"Somewhere in the mountains," he said, briefly. "His estates are there. He is said to be very rich and powerful. I know nothing more, signorini."

Realizing that little additional information could be gleaned from this source they soon left the shop and wandered into the Piazzo Vittorio Emanuele, and from thence by the narrow lane to the famous Teatro Greco.

For a time they admired this fascinating ruin, which has the best preserved stage of any Greek theatre now in existence. From the top of the hill is one of the most magnificent views in Sicily, and here our travellers sat in contemplative awe until Uncle John declared it was time to return to their hotel for luncheon.

As they passed the portiere's desk Mr. Merrick paused to ask that important official:

"Tell me, if you please, who is Signor Victor Valdi?"

"Valdi, signore?"

"Yes; the Duke di Valdi, I suppose you call him."

"I have never heard of him," replied the man.

"But every one seems to know him in Taormina."

"Is it so? We have but one duke near to us, and he--. But never mind. I do not know this Valdi."

"A thin faced man, with black eyes. We met him on the steamer coming from America."

The portiere dropped his eyes and turned toward his desk.

"Luncheon is served, signore," he remarked. "Also, here is a letter for you, which arrived this morning."

Uncle John took the letter and walked on to rejoin the girls.

"It seems hard work to find out anything about this Valdi," he said. "Either the folks here do not know him, or they won't acknowledge his acquaintance. We may as well follow suit, and avoid him."

"I don't like his looks a bit," observed Beth. "He seems afraid and defiant at the same time, and his temper is dreadful. It was only with great difficulty he could bring himself to be polite to us."

"Oh, I always got along with him all right," said Patsy. "I'm sure Signor Valdi isn't as bad as he appears. And he's a duke, too, girls--a real duke!"

"So it seems," Uncle John rejoined; "yet there is something queer about the fellow, I agree with Beth; I don't like him."

"Did Mr. Watson say when he would join us here?" enquired Louise, when they were seated at the little round table.

"No; but here's a letter from him. I'd quite forgotten it."

He tore open the envelope and carefully read the enclosure.

"Too bad," said he. "We might have stayed a few days in Messina. Watson says he and Kenneth have stopped at Girgenti--wherever that is--to study the temples. Wonder if they're Solomon's? They won't get to Taormina before Saturday."

"It won't matter," declared Patsy, "so long as they arrive then. And I'd a good deal rather be here than in Messina, or any other place. Of course we'll all be glad to see Kenneth."

"Mr. Watson wants us to be very careful while we are in Sicily," continued Uncle John, referring to the letter. "Listen to this: 'Don't let the girls wear jewelry in public places, or display their watches openly; and take care, all of you, not to show much money. If you buy anything, have it sent to your hotel to be paid for by the hall porter. And it is wise not to let anyone know who you are or how long you intend to remain in any one place. This may strike you as an absurd precaution; but you must remember that you are not in America, but in an isolated Italian province, where government control is inefficient. The truth is that the terrible Mafia is still all powerful on this island, and brigandage is by no means confined to the neighborhood of Castrogiovanni, as the guide books would have you believe. The people seem simple and harmless enough, but Kenneth and I always keep our revolvers handy, and believe it is a reasonable precaution. I don't want to frighten you, John; merely to warn you. Sicily is full of tourists, and few are ever molested; but if you are aware of the conditions underlying the public serenity you are not so liable to run yourself and your nieces into needless dangers.' How's that for a hair-curler, girls?"

"It sounds very romantic," said Louise, smiling. "Mr. Watson is such a cautious man!"

"But it's all rubbish about there being danger in Taormina," declared Patsy, indignantly. "Mr. Watson has been in the wilds of the interior, which Baedecker admits is infested with brigands. Here everyone smiles at us in the friendliest way possible."

"Except the duke," added Beth, with a laugh.

"Oh, the duke is sour by nature," Patsy answered; "but if there really was danger, I'm sure he'd protect us, for he lives here and knows the country."

"You are sure of a lot of things, dear," said her cousin, smiling. "But it will do no harm to heed the advice, and be careful."

They all agreed to that, and Uncle John was glad to remember he had two brand new revolvers in the bottom of his trunk, which he could use in an emergency if he could manage to find the cartridges to load them with.

He got them out next morning, and warned his nieces not to touch the dangerous things when they entered his room. But Patsy laughed at him, saying:

"You are behind the times, Uncle. Beth has carried a revolver ever since we started."

"Beth!" he cried, horrified.

"Just as a precaution," said that young lady, demurely.

"But you're only a child!"

"Even so, Uncle, I have been taught to shoot in Cloverton, as a part of my education. Once I won a medal--think of that! So I brought my pet revolver along, although I may never have need to use it."

Uncle John looked thoughtful.

"It doesn't seem like a girlish accomplishment, exactly," he mused. "When I was young and went into the West, the times were a bit unsettled, and I used to carry a popgun myself. But I never shot at a human being in my life. There were women in the camps that could shoot, too; but the safest place was always in front of them. If Beth has won a medal, though, she might hit something."

"Don't try, Beth," said Louise; "you ought to make a hit without shooting."

"Thank you, dear."

As they left their hotel for a walk they came upon Count Ferralti, who was standing in the court calmly smoking a cigarette. His right hand was still in a sling.

No one was greatly surprised at his appearance, but Uncle John uttered an exclamation of impatience. It annoyed him that this fellow, whose antecedents were decidedly cloudy, should be "chasing around" after one of his nieces, Beth and Patsy smiled at each other significantly as the young man was discovered, but Louise, with a slight blush, advanced to greet Ferralti in her usual pleasant and cordial way.

There was no use resenting the intrusion. They owed a certain consideration to this boyish Italian for his assistance on the Amalfi road. But Uncle John almost wished he had left them to escape as best they might, for the obligation was getting to be decidedly onerous.

While Ferralti was expressing his astonishment at so "unexpectedly" meeting again his American friends, Uncle John discovered their English speaking cocchiere, Frascatti Vietri, lolling half asleep on the box of his victoria.

"Would your energy like to drive us this morning?" he asked.

"It is my duty, signore, if you wish to go," was the reply.

"Then you are engaged. Come, girls; hop in, if you want to ride."

The three nieces and Uncle John just filled the victoria. The count was disconsolate at being so cleverly dropped from the party, but could only flourish his hat and wish them a pleasant drive.

They descended the winding road to the coast, where Frascatti took the highway to Sant' Alessio, a charming drive leading to the Taormina Pass.

"By the way," Uncle John asked the driver, "do you know of a duke that lives in this neighborhood?"

The laughing face of the Sicilian suddenly turned grave.

"No, signore. There is the Prince di Scaletta; but no duke on this side the town."

"But on the other side?"

"Oh; in the mountains? To be sure there are noblemen there; old estates almost forgotten in our great civilization of to-day. We are very progressive in Taormina, signore. There will be a fountain of the ice cream soda established next summer. Quite metropolitan, ne c'e?"

"Quite. But, tell me, Frascatti, have you a duke in the mountains back of Taormina?"

"Signore, I beg you to pay no attention to the foolish stories you may hear from our peasants. There has been no brigandage here for centuries. I assure you the country is perfectionly safe--especial if you stay within the town or take me on your drives. They know me, signore, and even Il Duca dares not trifle with my friends."

"Why should he, Frascatti, if there is no brigandage? Is it the Mafia?"

"Ah, I have heard that Mafia spoken of, but mostly when I lived in America, which is Chicago. Here we do not know of the Mafia."

"But you advise us to be careful?"

"Everywhere, illustrissimo signore, it is well to be what you call the circumspection. I remember that in the State street of Chicago, which is America, peaceful citizens were often killed by bandits. Eh, is it not so?"

"Quite probable," said Uncle John, soberly.

"Then, what will you? Are we worse than Americans, that you fear us? Never mind Il Duca, or the tales they foolishly whisper of him. Here you may be as safe and happy as in Chicago--which is America."

He turned to his horses and urged them up a slope. The girls and Uncle John eyed one another enquiringly.

"Our duke seems to bear no good reputation," said Beth, in a tone so low that Frascatti could not overhear. "Everyone fears to speak of him."

"Singular," said Uncle John, "that Patsy's friend turns out to be a mystery, even in his own home. I wonder if he is a leader of the Mafia, or just a common brigand?"

"In either case," said Patsy, "he will not care to injure us, I am sure. We all treated him very nicely, and I just made him talk and be sociable, whether he wanted to or not. That ought to count for something in our favor. But my opinion is that he's just a gruff old nobleman who lives in the hills and makes few friends."

"And hasn't a name, any more than Louise's count has. Is it customary, my dear, for all Italian noblemen to conceal their identity?"

"I do not know, Uncle," answered Louise, casting down her eyes.

CHAPTER XIV
UNCLE JOHN DISAPPEARS

Uncle John grew to love Taormina. Its wildness and ruggedness somehow reminded him of the Rockies in the old pioneer days, and he wandered through all the lanes of the quaint old town until he knew every cornice and cobblestone familiarly, and the women who sat weaving or mending before their squalid but picturesque hovels all nodded a greeting to the cheery little American as he passed by.

He climbed Malo, too, a high peak crowned by a ruined castle; and also Mt. Venere, on the plateau of which an ancient city had once stood. His walking tours did him good, and frequently while the girls lay stretched upon the grass that lined the theatre enclosure, to idle the time or read or write enthusiastic letters home, Uncle John, scorning such laziness, would take his stick and climb mountains, or follow the rough paths that diverged from the highway just beyond the Catania Gate.

The tax gatherer whose tiny office was just inside the gate came to know the little gentleman very well, and although he could speak no English he would bob his grizzled head and murmur: "Buon giorno, signore!" as the stranger passed out on his daily stroll.

One afternoon Mr. Merrick went down the hill path leading from the Castello-a-Mare to Capo di San Andrea, and as he passed around a narrow ledge of rock came full upon two men seated upon a flat stone. One was Valdi and the other Ferralti, and they seemed engaged in earnest conversation when he interrupted them. The Count smiled frankly and doffed his hat; the Duke frowned grimly, but also nodded.

Uncle John passed on. The path was wild and little frequented. He felt in his side pocket and grasped the handle of his revolver; but there was no attempt to follow or molest him. Nevertheless, when he returned from the beach he came up the longer winding roadway and was glad of the company of a ragged goatherd who, having no English, entertained "Il Signore" by singing ditties as he drove his goats before him.

The misgivings Uncle John had originally conceived concerning Count Ferralti returned in full force with this incident; but he resolved to say nothing of it to his nieces. Silas Watson would be with them in a couple of days more and he would consult the shrewd lawyer before he took any decisive action.

Next morning after breakfast he left his nieces in the garden and said he would take a walk through the town and along the highway west, toward Kaggi.

"I'll be back in an hour or so," he remarked, "for I have some letters to write and I want them to catch the noon mail."

So the girls sat on the terrace overlooking the sea and Etna, and breathed the sweet air and enjoyed the caressing sunshine, until they noticed the portiere coming hastily toward them.

"Pardon, signorini," he said, breathlessly, "but it will be to oblige me greatly if you will tell me where Signor Ferralti is."

"He is not of our party," answered Patsy, promptly; but Louise looked up as if startled, and said: "I have been expecting him to join us here."

"Then you do not know?" exclaimed the portiere, in an anxious tone.

"Know what, sir?" asked the girl.

"That Signor Ferralti is gone. He has not been seen by any after last evening. He did not occupy his room. But worse, far worse, will I break you the news gently--his baggage is gone with him!"

"His baggage gone!" echoed Louise, greatly disturbed. "And he did not tell you? You did not see him go?"

"Alas, no, signorina. His bill is still unsettled. He possessed two large travelling cases, which must have been carried out at the side entrance with stealth most deplorable. The padrone is worried. Signor Ferralti is American, and Americans seldom treat us wrongfully."

"Signor Ferralti is Italian," answered Louise, stiffly.

"The name is Italian, perhaps; but he speaks only the English," declared the portiere.

"He is not a rogue, however. Assure your master of that fact. When Mr. Merrick returns he will settle Count Ferralti's bill."

"Oh, Louise!" gasped Patsy.

"I don't understand it in the least," continued Louise, looking at her cousins as if she were really bewildered. "I left him in the courtyard last evening to finish his cigar, and he said he would meet us in the garden after breakfast. I am sure he had no intention of going away. And for the honor of American travellers his account here must be taken care of."

"One thing is singular," observed Beth, calmly. "There has been no train since last you saw him. If Count Ferralti has left the hotel, where could he be?"

The portiere brightened.

"Gia s'intende!" he exclaimed, "he must still be in Taormina--doubtless at some other hotel."

"Will you send and find out?" asked Louise.

"I will go myself, and at once," he answered. "And thank you, signorina, for the kind assurance regarding the account. It will relieve the padrone very much."

He hurried away again, and an uneasy silence fell upon the nieces.

"Do you care for this young man. Louise?" asked Beth, pointedly, after the pause had become awkward.

"He is very attentive and gentlemanly, and I feel you have all wronged him by your unjust suspicions," she replied, with spirit.

"That does not answer my question, dear," persisted her cousin. "Are you especially fond of him?"

"What right have you to question me in this way, Beth?"

"No right at all, dear. I am only trying to figure out our doubtful position in regard to this young man--a stranger to all of us but you."

"It is really none of our business," observed Patsy, quickly. "We're just a lot of gossips to be figuring on Count Ferralti at all. And although this sudden disappearance looks queer, on the face of it, the gentleman may simply have changed his boarding place."

"I do not think so," said Louise. "He liked this hotel very much."

"And he may have liked some of its guests," added Patsy, smiling. "Well, Uncle John will soon be back, and then we will talk it over with him."

Uncle John was late. The portiere returned first. He had been to every hotel in the little town, but none of them had received a guest since the afternoon train of yesterday. Count Ferralti had disappeared as if by magic, and no one could account for it.

Noon arrived, but no Uncle John. The girls became dispirited and anxious, for the little man was usually very prompt in keeping his engagements, and always had returned at the set time.

They waited until the last moment and then entered the salle a manger and ate their luncheon in gloomy silence, hoping every moment to hear the sound of their uncle's familiar tread.

After luncheon they held a hurried consultation and decided to go into town and search for him. So away they trooped, asking eager questions in their uncertain Italian but receiving no satisfactory reply until they reached the little office of the tax gatherer at the Catania Gate.

"Ah, si, signorini mia," he answered, cheerfully, "il poco signore passato da stamattini."

But he had not returned?

Not yet.

They looked at one another blankly.

"See here," said Patsy; "Uncle John must have lost his way or met with an accident. You go back to the hotel, Louise, and wait there in case he returns home another way. Beth and I will follow some of these paths and see if we can find him."

"He may have sprained an ankle, and be unable to walk," suggested Beth. "I think Patsy's advice is good."

So Louise returned through the town and the other girls began exploring the paths that led into the mountains from every turn of the highway. But although they searched eagerly and followed each path a mile or more of its length, no sign of life did they encounter--much less a sight of their missing uncle. The paths were wild and unfrequented, only on the Catania road itself a peasant now and then being found patiently trudging along or driving before him a donkey laden with panniers of oranges or lemons for the markets of Taormina.

On some of the solitary rocky paths they called to Uncle John by name, hoping that their voices might reach him; but only the echoes replied. Finally they grew discouraged.

"It will be sunset before we get back, even if we start this minute," said Beth, finally. "Let us return, and get some one to help us."

Patsy burst into tears.

"Oh, I'm sure he's lost, or murdered, or kidnapped!" she wailed. "Dear, dear Uncle John! Whatever shall we do, Beth?"

"Why, he may be at home, waiting for us to get back. Don't give way, Patsy; it will do no good, you know."

They were thoroughly tired when, just at sunset, they reached the hotel. Louise came to meet them, and by the question in her eyes they knew their uncle had not returned.

"Something must be done, and at once," said Beth, decidedly. She was the younger of the three girls, but in this emergency took the lead because of her calm and unruffled disposition and native good sense. "Is Frascatti in the courtyard?"

Patsy ran to see, and soon brought the vetturino into their sitting room. He could speak English and knew the neighborhood thoroughly. He ought to be able to advise them.

Frascatti listened intently to their story. He was very evidently impressed.

"Tell me, then, signorini," he said, thoughtfully; "is Senor Merreek very rich?"

"Why do you ask?" returned Beth, suspiciously. She remembered the warning conveyed in Mr. Watson's letter.

"Of course, I know that all the Americans who travel are rich," continued Frascatti. "I have myself been in Chicago, which is America. But is Signor Merreek a very rich and well acquainted man in his own country? Believe me, it is well that you answer truly."

"I think he is."

The man looked cautiously around, and then came nearer and dropped his voice to a whisper.

"Are you aware that Il Duca knows this?" he asked.

Beth thought a moment.

"We met the man you call Il Duca, but who told us he was Signor Victor Valdi, on board the ship, where many of the passengers knew my uncle well. If he listened to their conversation he would soon know all about John Merrick, of course."

Frascatti wagged his head solemnly.

"Then, signorina," he said, still speaking very softly, "I assure you there is no need to worry over your uncle's safety."

"What do you mean?" demanded Beth.

"People do not lose their way in our mountains," he replied. "The paths are straight, and lead all to the highways. And there is little danger of falling or of being injured. But--I regret to say it, signorini--it is a reflection upon our advanced civilization and the good name of our people--but sometimes a man who is rich disappears for a time, and no one knows how it is, or where he may be. He always returns; but then he is not so rich."

"I understand. My uncle is captured by brigands, you think."

"There are no brigands, signorina."

"Or the Mafia, then."

"I do not know the Mafia. All I know is that the very rich should keep their riches secret when they travel. In Chicago, which is America, they will knock you upon the head for a few miserable dollars; here my countrymen scorn to attack or to rob the common people. But when a man is so very rich that he does not need all of his money, there are, I regret to say, some lawless ones in Sicily who insist that he divide with them. But the prisoner is always well treated, and when he pays he is sent away very happy."

"Suppose he does not pay?"

"Ah, signorina, will not a drowning man clutch the raft that floats by? And the lawless ones do not take his all--merely a part."

The girls looked at one another helplessly.

"What must we do, Frascatti?" asked Patsy.

"Wait. In a day--two days, perhaps--you will hear from your uncle. He will tell you how to send money to the lawless ones. You will follow his instructions, and he will come home with smiles and singing. I know. It is very regrettable, but it is so."

"It will not be so in this case," said Beth, indignantly. "I will see the American consul--"

"I am sorry, but there is none here."

"I will telegraph to Messina for the military. They will search the mountains, and bring your brigands to justice."

Frascatti smiled sadly.

"Oh, yes; perhaps they will come. But the military is Italian--not Sicilian--and has no experience in these parts. The search will find nothing, except perhaps a dead body thrown upon the rocks to defy justice. It is very regrettable, signorina; but it is so."

Patsy was wringing her hands, frantic with terror. Louise was white and staring. Beth puckered her pretty brow in a frown and tried to think.

"Ferralti is also gone," murmured Louise, in a hoarse voice. "They will rob or murder him with Uncle John!"

"I am quite convinced," said Beth, coldly, "that your false count is a fellow conspirator of the brigand called Il Duca. He has been following us around to get a chance to ensnare Uncle John."

"Oh, no, no, Beth! It is not so! I know better than that."

"He would lie to you, of course," returned the girl bitterly. "As soon as the trap was set he disappeared, bag and baggage, and left the simple girl he had fooled to her own devices."

"You do not know what you are saying," retorted Louise, turning her back to Beth and walking to a window. From where they stood they could hear her sobbing miserably.

"Whether Frascatti is right or not," said Patsy, drying her eyes and trying to be brave, "we ought to search for Uncle John at once."

"I think so, too," agreed Beth. Then, turning to the Sicilian, she said: "Will you get together as many men as possible and search the hills, with lanterns, for my uncle? You shall be well paid for all you do."

"Most certainly, signorina, if it will please you," he replied. "How long do you wish us to search?"

"Until you find him."

"Then must we grow old in your service. Non fa niente! It is regrettable, but--"

"Will you go at once?" stamping her foot angrily.

"Most certainly, signorina."

"Then lose no time. I will go with you and see you start."

She followed the man out, and kept at his side until he had secured several servants with lanterns for the search. The promise of high caparra or earnest money made all eager to join the band, but the padrone could only allow a half dozen to leave their stations at the hotel. In the town, however, whither Beth accompanied them, a score of sleepy looking fellows were speedily secured, and under the command of Frascatti, who had resolved to earn his money by energy and good will because there was no chance of success, they marched out of the Catania Gate and scattered along the mountain paths.

"If you find Uncle John before morning I will give you a thousand lira additional," promised Beth.

"We will search faithfully," replied her captain, "but the signorina must not be disappointed if the lawless ones evade us. They have a way of hiding close in the caves, where none may find them. It is regrettable, very; but it is so."

Then he followed his men to the mountains, and as the last glimmer from his lantern died away the girl sighed heavily and returned alone through the deserted streets to the hotel.

Clouds hid the moon and the night was black and forbidding; but it did not occur to her to be afraid.

CHAPTER XV
DAYS OF ANXIETY

Uncle John's nieces passed a miserable night. Patsy stole into his room and prayed fervently beside his bed that her dear uncle might be preserved and restored to them in health and safety. Beth, meantime, paced the room she shared with Patsy with knitted brows and flashing eyes, the flush in her cheeks growing deeper as her anger increased. An ungovernable temper was the girl's worst failing; the abductors of her uncle were arousing in her the most violent passions of which she was capable, and might lead her to adopt desperate measures. She was only a country girl, and little experienced in life, yet Beth might be expected to undertake extraordinary things if, as she expressed it, if she "got good and mad!"

No sound was heard during the night from the room occupied by Louise, but the morning disclosed a white, drawn face and reddened eyelids as proof that she had rested as little as her cousins.

Yet, singularly enough, Louise was the most composed of the three when they gathered in the little sitting room at daybreak, and tried earnestly to cheer the spirits of her cousins. Louise never conveyed the impression of being especially sincere, but the pleasant words and manners she habitually assumed rendered her an agreeable companion, and this faculty of masking her real feelings now stood her in good stead and served to relieve the weight of anxiety that oppressed them all.

Frascatti came limping back with his tired followers in the early dawn, and reported that no trace of the missing man had been observed. There were no brigands and no Mafia; on that point all his fellow townsmen agreed with him fully. But it was barely possible some lawless ones who were all unknown to the honest Taorminians had made the rich American a prisoner.

Il Duca? Oh, no, signorini! A thousand times, no. Il Duca was queer and unsociable, but not lawless. He was of noble family and a native of the district. It would be very wrong and foolish to question Il Duca's integrity.

With this assertion Frascatti went to bed. He had not shirked the search, because he was paid for it, and he and his men had tramped the mountains faithfully all night, well knowing it would result in nothing but earning their money.

On the morning train from Catania arrived Silas Watson and his young ward Kenneth Forbes, the boy who had so unexpectedly inherited Aunt Jane's fine estate of Elmhurst on her death. The discovery of a will which gave to Kenneth all the property their aunt had intended for her nieces had not caused the slightest estrangement between the young folks, then or afterward. On the contrary, the girls were all glad that the gloomy, neglected boy, with his artistic, high-strung temperament, would be so well provided for. Without the inheritance he would have been an outcast; now he was able to travel with his guardian, the kindly old Elmhurst lawyer, and fit himself for his future important position in the world. More than all this, however, Kenneth had resolved to be a great landscape painter, and Italy and Sicily had done much, in the past year, to prepare him for this career.

The boy greeted his old friends with eager delight, not noticing for the moment their anxious faces and perturbed demeanor. But the lawyer's sharp eyes saw at once that something was wrong.

"Where is John Merrick?" he asked.

"Oh, I'm so glad you've come!" cried Patsy, clinging to his hand.

"We are in sore straits, indeed, Mr. Watson," said Louise.

"Uncle John is lost," explained Beth, "and we're afraid he is in the hands of brigands."

Then she related as calmly as she could all that had happened. The relation was clear and concise. She told of their meeting with Valdi on the ship, of Count Ferralti's persistence in attaching himself to their party, and of Uncle John's discovery that the young man was posing under an assumed name. She did not fail to mention Ferralti's timely assistance on the Amalfi drive, or his subsequent devoted attentions to Louise; but the latter Beth considered merely as an excuse for following them around.

"In my opinion," said she, "we have been watched ever since we left America, by these two spies, who had resolved to get Uncle John into some unfrequented place and then rob him. If they succeed in their vile plot, Mr. Watson, we shall be humiliated and disgraced forever."

"Tut-tut," said he; "don't think of that. Let us consider John Merrick, and nothing else."

Louise protested that Beth had not been fair in her conclusions. The Count was an honorable man; she would vouch for his character herself.

But Mr. Watson did not heed this defense. The matter was very serious--how serious he alone realized--and his face was grave indeed as he listened to the descriptions of that terrible Il Duca whom the natives all shrank from and refused to discuss.

When he had learned all the nieces had to tell he hastened into the town and telegraphed the American consul at Messina. Then he found the questura, or police office, and was assured by the officer in attendance that the disappearance of Mr. Merrick was already known to the authorities and every effort was being made to find him.

"Do you think he has been abducted by brigands?" asked the lawyer.

"Brigands, signore?" was the astonished reply. "There are no brigands in this district at all. We drove them out many years ago."

"How about Il Duca?"

"And who is that, signore?"

"Don't you know?"

"I assure you we have no official knowledge of such a person. There are dukes in Sicily, to be sure; but 'Il Duca' means nothing. Perhaps you can tell me to whom you refer?"

"See here," said the lawyer, brusquely; "I know your methods, questore mia, but they won't prove effective in this case. If you think an American is helpless in this country you are very much mistaken. But, to save time, I am willing to submit to your official requirements. I will pay you well for the rescue of my friend."

"All shall be done that is possible."

"But if you do not find him at once, and return him to us unharmed, I will have a regiment of soldiers in Taormina to search your mountains and break up the bands of brigands that infest them. When I prove that brigands are here and that you were not aware of them, you will be disgraced and deposed from your office."

The official shrugged his shoulders, a gesture in which the Sicilian is as expert as the Frenchman.

"I will welcome the soldiery," said he; "but you will be able to prove nothing. The offer of a reward may accomplish more--if it is great enough to be interesting."

"How great is that?"

"Can I value your friend? You must name the reward yourself. But even then I can promise nothing. In the course of our duty every effort is now being made to find the missing American. But we work in the dark, as you know. Your friend may be a suicide; he may have lost his mind and wandered into the wilderness; he may have committed some crime and absconded. How do I know? You say he is missing, but that is no reason the brigands have him, even did brigands exist, which I doubt. Rest assured, signore, that rigid search will be made. It is my boast that I leave no duty unfulfilled."

Mr. Watson walked back to the telegraph office and found an answer to his message. The American consul was ill and had gone to Naples for treatment. When he returned, his clerk stated, the matter of the disappearance of John Merrick would immediately be investigated.

Feeling extremely helpless and more fearful for his friend than before, the lawyer returned to the hotel for a conference with the nieces.

"How much of a reward shall I offer?" he asked. "That seems to be the only thing that can be depended upon to secure results."

"Give them a million--Uncle John won't mind," cried Patsy, earnestly.

"Don't give them a penny, sir," said Beth. "If they are holding him for a ransom Uncle is in no personal danger, and we have no right to assist in robbing him."

"But you don't understand, my dear," asserted the lawyer. "These brigands never let a victim go free unless they are well paid. That is why they are so often successful. If John Merrick is not ransomed he will never again be heard of."

"But this is not a ransom, sir. You propose to offer a reward to the police."

"Let me explain. The ways of the Italian police are very intricate. They know of no brigandage here, and cannot find a brigand. But if the reward is great enough to divide, they know where to offer a share of it, in lieu of a ransom, and will force the brigands to accept it. In that way the police gets the glory of a rescue and a share of the spoils. If we offer no reward, or an insignificant one, the brigands will be allowed to act as they please."

"That is outrageous!" exclaimed Beth.

"Yes. The Italian government deplores it. It is trying hard to break up a system that has existed for centuries, but has not yet succeeded."

"Then I'd prefer to deal directly with the brigands."

"So would I, if--"

"If what, sir?"

"If we were sure your uncle is in their hands. Do you think the party you sent out last night searched thoroughly?"

"I hope so."

"I will send out more men at once. They shall search the hills in every direction. Should they find nothing our worst fears will be confirmed, and then--"

"Well, Mr. Watson?"

"Then we must wait for the brigands to dictate the terms of a ransom, and make the best bargain we can."

"That seems sensible," said Kenneth, and both Patsy and Louise agreed with him, although it would be tedious waiting.

But Beth only bit her lip and frowned.

Mr. Watson's searching party was maintained all day--for two days, and three; but without result. Then they waited for the brigands to act. But a week dragged painfully by and no word of John Merrick's whereabouts reached the ears of the weary watchers.

CHAPTER XVI
TATO

When Uncle John passed through the west gate for a tramp along the mountain paths he was feeling in an especially happy and contented mood. The day was bright and balmy, the air bracing, the scenery unfolded step by step magnificent and appealing. To be in this little corner of the old world, amid ruins antedating the Christian era, and able to wholly forget those awful stock and market reports of Wall street, was a privilege the old gentleman greatly appreciated.

So away he trudged, exploring this path or that leading amongst the rugged cliffs, until finally he began to take note of his erratic wanderings and wonder where he was. Climbing an elevated rock near the path he poised himself upon its peak and studied the landscape spread out beneath him.

There was a patch of sea, with the dim Calabrian coast standing sentry behind it. The nearer coast was hidden from view, but away at the left was a dull white streak marking the old wall of Taormina, and above this the ruined citadel and the ancient castle of Mola--each on its separate peak.

"I must be getting back," he thought, and sliding down the surface of the rock he presently returned to the path from whence he had climbed.

To his surprise he found a boy standing there and looking at him with soft brown eyes that were both beautiful and intelligent. Uncle John was as short as he was stout, but the boy scarcely reached to his shoulder. He was slender and agile, and clothed in a grey corduroy suit that was better in texture than the American had seen other Sicilian youths wear. As a rule the apparel of the children in this country seemed sadly neglected.

Yet the most attractive thing about this child was his face, which was delicate of contour, richly tinted to harmonize with his magnificent brown eyes, and so sensitive and expressive that it seemed able to convey the most subtle shades of emotion. He seemed ten or twelve years of age, but might have been much older.

As soon as the American had returned to the path the boy came toward him in an eager, excited way, and exclaimed:

"Is it not Signor Merrick?"

The English was fluent, and only rendered softer by the foreign intonation.

"It is," said Uncle John, cheerfully. "Where did you drop from, my lad? I thought these hills were deserted, until now."

"I am sent by a friend," answered the boy, speaking rapidly and regarding the man with appealing glances. "He is in much trouble, signore, and asks your aid."

"A friend? Who is it?"

"The name he gave me is Ferralti, signore. He is near to this place, in the hills yonder, and unable to return to the town without assistance."

"Ferralti. H-m-m. Is he hurt?"

"Badly, signore; from a fall on the rocks."

"And he sent for me?"

"Yes, signore. I know you by sight--who does not?--and as I hurried along I saw you standing on the rock. It is most fortunate. Will you hasten to your friend, then? I will lead you to him."

Uncle John hesitated. He ought to be getting home, instead of penetrating still farther into these rocky fastnesses. And Ferralti was no especial friend, to claim his assistance. But then the thought occurred that this young Italian had befriended both him and his nieces in an extremity, and was therefore entitled to consideration when trouble in turn overtook himself. The natural impulse of this thought was to go to his assistance.

"All right, my lad," said he. "Lead on, and I'll see what can be done for Ferralti. Is it far?"

"Not far, signore."

With nervous, impatient steps the child started up the narrow path and Uncle John followed--not slowly, but scarcely fast enough to satisfy his zealous guide.

"What is your name, little one?"

"Tato, signore."

"Where do you live?"

"Near by, signore."

"And how did you happen to find Ferralti?"

"By chance, signore."

Uncle John saved his remaining breath for the climb. He could ask questions afterward.

The path was in a crevasse where the rocks seemed once to have split. It was narrow and steep, and before long ended in a cul de sac. The little man thought they had reached their destination, then; but without hesitation the boy climbed over a boulder and dropped into another path on the opposite side, holding out a hand to assist the American.

Uncle John laughed at the necessity, but promptly slid his stout body over the boulder and then paused to mop his brow.

"Much farther, Tato?"

"Just a step, signore."

"It is lucky you found Ferralti, or he might have died in these wilds without a soul knowing he was here."

"That is true, signore."

"Well, is this the path?"

"Yes, signore. Follow me, please."

The cliffs were precipitous on both sides of them. It was another crevasse, but not a long one. Presently the child came to a halt because the way ended and they could proceed no farther. He leaned against the rock and in a high-pitched, sweet voice sang part of a Sicilian ditty, neither starting the verse nor ending it, but merely trilling out a fragment.

Uncle John regarded him wonderingly; and then, with a sudden suspicion, he demanded:

"You are not playing me false, Tato?"

"I, signore?" smiling frankly into the man's eyes; "you need never fear Tato, signore. To be your friend, and Signor Ferralti's friend, makes me very proud."

The rock he leaned against fell inward, noiselessly, and disclosed a passage. It was short, for there was light at the other end.

The strange child darted in at once.

"This way, signore. He is here!"

Uncle John drew back. He had forgotten until now that these mountains are dangerous. And something strange in the present proceedings, the loneliness of the place and the elfish character of his guide, suddenly warned him to be cautious.

"See here, my lad," he called: "I'll go no farther."

Instantly Tato was at his side again, grasping the man's hand in his tiny brown one and searching his face with pleading eyes.

"Ah, signore, you will not fail your friend, when he is so near you and in such great trouble? See! I who am a stranger and not even his countryman, even I weep for the poor young man, and long to comfort him. Do you, his friend, refuse him aid because you have fear of the wild mountains and a poor peasant boy?"

Tears really stood in the beautiful brown eyes. They rolled down his cheeks, as with both hands he pressed that of Uncle John and urged him gently forward.

"Oh, well; lead on, Tato. I'll see the other side of your tunnel, anyhow. But if you play me tricks, my lad--"

He paused, for a wonderful vision had opened before him. Coming through the short passage hewn in the rocks the American stood upon a ledge facing a most beautiful valley, that was hemmed in by precipitous cliffs on every side. From these stern barriers of the outside world the ground sloped gradually toward the center, where a pretty brook flowed, its waters sparkling like diamonds in the sunlight as it tumbled over its rocky bed. Groves of oranges and of olive, lemon and almond trees occupied much of the vale, and on a higher point at the right, its back to the wall of rock that towered behind it, stood a substantial yet picturesque mansion of stone, with several outbuildings scattered on either side.

The valley seemed, indeed, a toy kingdom sequestered from the great outside world, yet so rich and productive within itself that it was independent of all else.

Uncle John gazed with amazement. Who could have guessed this delightful spot was hidden safe within the heart of the bleak, bare mountain surrounding it? But suddenly he bethought himself.

"What place is this, Tato?" he asked; "and where is our friend Ferralti, who needs me?"

There was no reply.

He turned around to find the boy had disappeared. Moreover, the passage had disappeared. Only a wall of rock was behind him, and although his eyes anxiously searched the rifts and cracks of its rough surface, no indication of the opening through which he had passed could be discovered.

CHAPTER XVII
THE HIDDEN VALLEY

Uncle John's first inspiration was to sit down upon a stone to think. He drew out his pipe and lighted it, to assist his meditations.

These were none too pleasant. That he had been cleverly entrapped, and that by a child scarcely in its teens, was too evident to need reflection. And what a secure trap it was! The mountains ranged all around the valley were impossible to scale, even by an Alpine climber, and to one who was not informed of its location the existence of the valley itself was unimaginable.

"I had not believed Ferralti was so shrewd," he muttered, wonderingly. "That something was wrong about the fellow I knew, of course; but I had not suspected such a thing as this. Now, then, first of all let me mark this spot, so that I will remember it. Just back of where I now stand is the entrance or outlet to the tunnel through the wall. It is closed, I suppose, by a swinging stone, like the one on the opposite side. I saw that one opened--opened by some person concealed from view, as soon as the boy sang his bit of song which was the signal agreed upon. And I was fool enough, after that warning, to walk straight through the tunnel! You're getting old, John Merrick; that's the only way I can account for your folly. But Ferralti hasn't won the odd trick yet, and if I keep my wits about me he isn't likely to win."

Thus ruminating, Uncle John searched the rocky wall carefully and believed he would know the place again, although which of the rough stones of its surface formed the doorway to the tunnel he could not guess.

A ledge of rock served as a path leading to right and left around this end of the valley, or "pocket" in the mountain, as it could more properly be called. Uncle John turned to the right, striding along with his usual deliberation, smoking his pipe and swinging his cane as he approached the stone dwelling that formed the center of the little settlement. As yet no sign of human life had he observed since Tato had disappeared, although a few cows were standing in a green meadow and some goats scrambled among the loose rocks at the further end of the enclosure.

Around the house the grounds had been laid out in gardens, with flowers and shrubbery, hedges and shade trees scattered about. Chickens clucked and strutted along the paths and an air of restfulness and peace brooded over all.

Uncle John was plainly mystified until he drew quite close to the dwelling, which had many verandas and balconies and bore every evidence of habitation. Then, to his astonishment, he beheld the form of a man stretched lazily in a wicker chair beside the entrance, and while he paused, hesitating, the man sat up and bowed politely to him.

"Good morning, Signor Merreek."

It was Victor Valdi, or, ignoring the fictitious name, the mysterious personage known as "Il Duca."

"Behold my delight, Signor Merreek, to receive you in my poor home," continued the man. "Will you not be seated, caro amico?"

The words were soft and fair, but the dark eyes gleamed with triumph and a sneer curled the thin lips.

"Thank you," said Uncle John; "I believe I will."

He stepped upon the veranda and sat down opposite his host.

"I came to see Count Ferralti, who is hurt, I understand," he continued.

"It is true, signore, but not badly. The poor count is injured mostly in his mind. Presently you shall see him."

"No hurry," observed Uncle John. "Pleasant place you have here, Duke."

"It is very good of you to praise it, signore. It is my most ancient patrimony, and quite retired and exclusive."

"So I see."

"The house you have honored by your presence, signore, was erected some three hundred and thirty years ago, by an ancestor who loved retirement. It has been in my family ever since. We all love retirement."

"Very desirable spot for a brigand, I'm sure," remarked the American, puffing his pipe composedly.

"Brigand? Ah, it pleases you to have humor, signore, mia. Brigand! But I will be frank. It is no dishonor to admit that my great ancestors of past centuries were truly brigands, and from this quiet haven sallied forth to do mighty deeds. They were quite famous, I am told, those olden Dukes d'Alcanta."

"I do not question it."

"Our legends tell of how my great ancestors demanded tribute of the rich who passed through their domain--for all this end of Sicily was given to us by Peter of Aragon, and remained in our possession until the second Ferdinand robbed us of it. Those times were somewhat wild and barbarous, signore, and a gentleman who protected his estates and asked tribute of strangers was termed a brigand, and became highly respected. But now it is different. We are civilized and meek, and ruled most lovingly by Italy. They will tell you there is no brigandage in all Sicily."

"So I understand."

"To-day I am nobody. My very name is forgotten. Those around this mountain know nothing of my little estate, and I am content. I desire not glory: I desire not prominence; to live my life in seclusion, with the occasional visit of a friend like yourself, is enough to satisfy me."

"You seem well known in Taormina."

"Quite a mistake, signore."

"And the natives must have climbed these peaks at times and looked down into your secluded kingdom."

"If so, they have forgotten it."

"I see."

"I give to the churches and the poor, but in secret. If I have an enemy, he disappears--I do not know how; no one knows."

"Of course not. You are an improvement on your ancestors, Duke. Instead of being a brigand you belong to the Mafia, and perform your robberies and murders in security. Very clever, indeed."

"But again you are wrong, signore," replied the Duke, with a frown. "I have never known of this Mafia, of which you speak, nor do I believe it exists. For myself, I am no robber, but a peaceful merchant."

"A merchant?" returned Uncle John, surprised by the statement.

"To be sure. I have some ancient and very valuable relics in my possession, treasured most carefully from the mediæval days. These I sell to my friends--who are fortunately all foreigners like yourself and can appreciate such treasures--and so obtain for myself and my family a modest livelihood."

"And you expect to sell something to me?" asked Uncle John, understanding very well the Sicilian's meaning.

"It is my earnest hope, signore."

The American fell silent, thinking upon the situation. The fierce looking brigand beside him was absurd enough, in his way, but doubtless a dangerous man to deal with. Uncle John was greatly interested in the adventure. It was such a sharp contrast to the hum-drum, unromantic American life he had latterly known that he derived a certain enjoyment from the novel experience. If the girls did not worry over his absence he would not much regret his visit to Il Duca's secluded valley.

It was already midday, and his nieces would be expecting him to luncheon. When he did not appear they would make enquiries, and try to find him. It occurred to him how futile all such attempts must prove. Even to one acquainted with the mountain paths the entrance to the duke's domain was doubtless a secret, and the brigand had plainly hinted that the native Sicilians were too cautious to spy upon him or molest him in any way.

So far, the only person he had seen was Il Duca himself. The child who had decoyed him was, of course, somewhere about, and so also was Ferralti. How many servants or followers the brigand might have was as yet a mystery to the new arrival.

In the side pocket of Uncle John's loose coat lay a loaded revolver, which he had carried ever since he had received Mr. Watson's warning letter. He had never imagined a condition of danger where he could not use this weapon to defend himself, and as long as it remained by him he had feared nothing. But he had been made a prisoner in so deft a manner that he had no opportunity to expostulate or offer any sort of resistance. Later there might be a chance to fight for his liberty, and the only sensible action was to wait and bide his time.

"For example," the Duke was saying, in his labored, broken English, "I have here a priceless treasure--very antique, very beautiful. It was in one time owned by Robert the Norman, who presented it to my greatest ancestor."

He drew an odd-shaped ring from his pocket and handed it to the American. It was of dull gold and set with a half dozen flat-cut garnets. Perhaps antique; perhaps not; but of little intrinsic value.

"This ring I have decided to sell, and it shall be yours, Signor Merreek, at a price far less than is represented by its historic worth. I am sure you will be glad to buy it."

"For how much?" asked Uncle John, curiously.

"A trifle; a mere hundred thousand lira."

"Twenty thousand dollars!"

"The ring of King Roger. How cheap! But, nevertheless, you shall have it for that sum."

Uncle John smiled.

"My dear Duke," he replied, "you have made a sad mistake. I am a comparatively poor man. My fortune is very modest."

The brigand lay back in his chair and lighted a fresh cigarette.

"I fear you undervalue yourself, my dear guest," he said. "Recently have I returned from America, where I was told much of the wealth of Signor John Merreek, who is many times a millionaire. See," drawing a paper from his pocket, "here is a list of the stocks and securities you own. Also of government and railway bonds, of real estate and of manufactures controlled by your money. I will read, and you will correct me if an error occurs."

Uncle John listened and was amazed. The schedule was complete, and its total was many millions. It was a better list of holdings than Uncle John possessed himself.

"You foreigners make queer mistakes, Duke," said he, taking another tack. "This property belongs to another John Merrick. It is a common name, and that is doubtless why you mistook me for the rich John Merrick."

"I have noticed," returned the Duke, coldly, "that this strange delusion of mind is apt to overtake my guests. But do not be alarmed; it will pass away presently, and then you will realize that you are yourself. Remember that I crossed the Atlantic on your steamship, signore. Many people there on board spoke of you and pointed you out to me as the great man of finance. Your own niece that is called Patsy, she also told me much about you, and of your kindness to her and the other young signorini. Before I left New York a banker of much dignity informed me you would sail on the ship 'Princess Irene.' If a mistake has been made, signore, it is yours, and not mine. Is your memory clearer now?"

Uncle John laughed frankly. The rascal was too clever for him to dispute with.

"Whoever I am," said he, "I will not buy your ring."

"I am pained," replied the brigand, lightly. "But there is ample time for you to reflect upon the matter. Do not decide hastily, I implore you. I may have been too liberal in making my offer, and time may assist me in fixing a just price for the relic. But we have had enough of business just now. It is time for our midday collation. Oblige me by joining us, signore."

He blew a shrill whistle, and a man stepped out of a doorway. He was an enormous Sicilian, tall, sinewy and with a countenance as dark and fierce as his master's. In his belt was a long knife, such as is known as a stilleto.

"Tommaso," said the Duke, "kindly show Signor Merreek to his room, and ask Guido if luncheon is ready to be served."

"Va bene, padrone," growled the man, and turned obediently to escort the American.

Uncle John entered the house, traversed a broad and cool passage, mounted to the second floor and found himself in a pleasant room with a balcony overlooking the valley. It was comfortably furnished, and with a bow that was not without a certain grim respect the man left him alone and tramped down the stairs again. There had been no attempt to restrain his liberty or molest him in any way, yet he was not slow to recognize the fact that he was a prisoner. Not in the house, perhaps, but in the valley. There was no need to confine him more closely. He could not escape.

He bathed his hands and face, dried them on a fresh towel, and found his toilet table well supplied with conveniences. In the next room some one was pacing the floor like a caged beast, growling and muttering angrily at every step.

Uncle John listened. "The brigand seems to have more than one guest," he thought, and smiled at the other's foolish outbursts.

Then he caught a word or two of English that made him start. He went to the door between the two rooms and threw it open, finding himself face to face with Count Ferralti.

CHAPTER XVIII
GUESTS OF THE BRIGAND

"Good morning, Count," said Uncle John, cheerfully.

The other stared at him astonished.

"Good heavens! Have they got you, too?" he exclaimed.

"Why, I'm visiting his excellency, Il Duca, if that's what you mean," replied Mr. Merrick. "But whether he's got me, or I've got him, I haven't yet decided."

The young man's jaw was tied in a bandage and one of his eyes was black and discolored. He looked agitated and miserable.

"Sir, you are in grave danger; we are both in grave danger," he announced, "unless we choose to submit to being robbed by this rascally brigand."

"Then," observed Uncle John, "let's submit."

"Never! Not in a thousand years!" cried Ferralti, wildly. And then this singular young man sank into a chair and burst into tears.

Uncle John was puzzled. The slender youth--for he was but a youth in spite of his thin moustaches--exhibited a queer combination of courage and weakness; but somehow Uncle John liked him better at that moment than he ever had before. Perhaps because he now realized he had unjustly suspected him.

"You seem to have been hurt, Count," he remarked.

"Why, I was foolish enough to struggle, and that brute Tommaso pounded me," was the reply. "You were wise to offer no resistance, sir."

"As for that, I hadn't a choice," said Uncle John, smiling. "When did they get you, Ferralti?"

"Last evening. I walked in the garden of the hotel and they threw a sack over my head. I resisted and tried to cry out. They beat me until I was insensible and then brought me here, together with my travelling cases, which they removed from my room to convey the impression that I had gone away voluntarily. When I awakened from my swoon I was in this room, with the doctor bending over me."

"The doctor?"

"Oh, they have a doctor in this accursed den, as well as a priest and a lawyer. The Duke entreated my pardon. He will punish his men for abusing me. But he holds me a safe prisoner, just the same."

"Why?"

"He wants a ransom. He will force me to purchase an ancient brass candlestick for fifty thousand lira."

Uncle John looked at his companion thoughtfully.

"Tell me, Count Ferralti," he said, "who you really are. I had believed you were Il Duca's accomplice, until now. But if he has trapped you, and demands a ransom, it is because you are a person of some consequence, and able to pay. May I not know as much about your position in life as does this brigand duke?"

The young man hesitated. Then he spread out his hands with an appealing gesture and said:

"Not yet, Mr. Merrick! Do not press me now, I implore you. Perhaps I have done wrong to try to deceive you, but in good time I will explain everything, and then you will understand me better."

"You are no count."

"That is true, Mr. Merrick."

"You are not even an Italian."

"That is but partly true, sir."

"You have seen fit to deceive us by--"

Tommaso threw wide the door.

"Il dejuné é servito," he said gruffly.

"What does that mean?" asked Uncle John.

"Luncheon is ready. Shall we go down?"

"Yes; I'm hungry."

They followed the man to the lower floor, where he ushered them into a low, cool room where a long table was set. The walls were whitewashed and bore some religious prints, gaudily colored. A white cloth covered the table, which was well furnished with modern crockery and glass, and antique silverware.

At the head of the table were two throne-like chairs, one slightly larger and more elevated than the other. In the more important seat was a withered old woman with a face like that of a mummy, except that it was supplied with two small but piercing jet eyes that seemed very much alive as they turned shrewdly upon the strangers. She was the only one of the company they found seated. The Duke stood behind the smaller chair beside her, and motioned the Americans to occupy two places at the side of the table next him. Opposite them, in the places adjoining the elevated dais, were two remarkable individuals whom Uncle John saw for the first time. One was a Cappuccin monk, with shaven crown and coarse cassock fastened at the waist by a cord. He was blind in one eye and the lid of the other drooped so as to expose only a thin slit. Fat, awkward and unkempt, he stood holding to the back of his chair and swaying slightly from side to side. Next to him was a dandified appearing man who was very slight and thin of form but affected the dress and manners of extreme youth. Ferralti whispered to Uncle John that this was the doctor.

The table dropped a step in heighth from these places, and the balance of its length was occupied by several stalwart Sicilians, clothed in ordinary peasant costume, and a few silent, heavy-featured women. Tato was not present.

"Signori," said the Duke to the Americans, "allow me to present you to my mother, the head of our illustrious family; one who is known, admired and feared throughout Sicily as her Excellenza la Duchessa d'Alcanta."

With the words the Duke bowed low to the old woman. Uncle John and Ferralti also bowed low. The lines of servitors humbly bent themselves double. But the Duchessa made no acknowledgment. Her bead like eyes searched the faces of the "guests" with disconcerting boldness, and then dropped to her plate.

At this signal the fat priest mumbled a blessing upon the food, the Duke waved his hand, and all the company became seated.

Uncle John felt as if he were taking part in a comic opera, and enjoyed the scene immensely. But now his attention was distracted by the stewards bringing in steaming platters of macaroni and stewed mutton, from which they first served the Duchessa, and then the Duke, and afterward the guests. The servants waited hungry-eyed until these formalities were completed, and then swept the platters clean and ate ravenously.

Uncle John plied his knife and fork busily and found the food excellently prepared. Ferralti seemed to have little appetite. Some of his teeth had been knocked out and his broken wrist, which had but partially healed, had been wrenched in the scrimmage of the night before so that it caused him considerable pain.

The Duke attempted little conversation, doubtless through deference to the aged Duchessa, who remained absolutely silent and unresponsive to her surroundings. He praised his wine, however, which he said was from their own vineyards, and pressed the Americans to drink freely.

When she had finished her meal the Duchessa raised a hand, and at the signal the whole company arose and stood at their places while two of the women assisted her to retire. She leaned upon their shoulders, being taller than her son, but displayed surprising vigor for one so advanced in years.

When she had gone the others finished at their leisure, and the conversation became general, the servants babbling in their voluble Italian without any restraint whatever.

Then the Duke led his prisoners to the veranda and offered them cigars. These were brought by Tato, who then sat in the duke's lap and curled up affectionately in his embrace, while the brigand's expression softened and he stroked the boy's head with a tender motion.

Uncle John watched the little scene approvingly. It was the first time he had seen Tato since the child had lured him through the tunnel.

"Your son, Duke?" he asked.

"Yes, signore; my only child. The heir to my modest estate."

"And a very good brigand, already, for his years," added Mr. Merrick. "Ah, Tato, Tato," shaking his head at the child, "how could you be so cruel as to fool an innocent old chap like me?"

Tato laughed.

"I did not deceive you, signore. You but misunderstood me. I said Signor Ferralti was hurt, and so he was."

"But you said he needed my assistance."

"Does he not, signore?"

"How do you speak such good English?"

"Father Antoine taught me."

"The monk?"

"Yes, signore."

"My child is a linguist," remarked the Duke, complacently. "Sh--he has been taught English, German and French, even from the days of infancy. It is very good for me, for now Tato can entertain my guests."

"Have you no Italian guests, then?" asked Uncle John.

"No, since Italy owns Sicily, and I am a loyal subject. Neither have I many Germans or Frenchmen, although a few wander my way, now and then. But the Americans I love, and often they visit me. There were three last year, and now here are two more to honor me with their presence."

"The Americans make easier victims, I suppose."

"Oh, the Americans are very rich, and they purchase my wares liberally. By the way, Signor Ferralti," turning to the young man, "have you decided yet the little matter of your own purchase?"

"I will not buy your candlestick, if that is what you refer to," was the response.

"No?"

"By no means. Fifty thousand lira, for a miserable bit of brass!"

"But I forgot to tell you, signore; the candlestick is no longer for sale," observed the Duke, with an evil smile. "Instead, I offer you a magnificent bracelet which is a hundred years old."

"Thank you. What's the price?"

"A hundred thousand lira, signore."

Ferralti started. Then in turn he smiled at his captor.

"That is absurd," said he. "I have no wealth at all, sir, but live on a small allowance that barely supplies my needs. I cannot pay."

"I will take that risk, signore," said the brigand, coolly. "You have but to draw me an order on Mr. Edward Leighton, of New York, for one hundred thousand lira--or say twenty thousand dollars--and the bracelet is yours."

"Edward Leighton! My father's attorney! How did you know of him, sir?"

"I have an agent in New York," answered the Duke, "and lately I have been in your city myself."

"Then, if you know so much, you scoundrelly thief, you know that my father will not honor a draft for such a sum as you demand. I doubt if my father would pay a single dollar to save me from assassination."

"We will not discuss that, signore, for I regret to say that your father is no longer able to honor drafts. However, your attorney can do so, and will, without question."

Ferralti stared at him blankly.

"What do you mean by that?" he demanded.

The Duke shook the ashes from his cigar and examined the glowing end with interest.

"Your father," was the deliberate reply, "was killed in a railway accident, four days ago. I have just been notified of the fact by a cable from America."

Ferralti sat trembling and regarding the man with silent horror.

"Is this true, sir?" asked Uncle John, quickly; "or is it only a part of your cursed game?"

"It is quite true, signore, I regret being obliged to break the ill news so abruptly; but this gentleman thought himself too poor to purchase my little bracelet, and it was necessary to inform him that he is suddenly made wealthy--not yet so great a Croesus as yourself, Signor Merreek, but still a very rich man."

Ferralti ceased trembling, but the horror still clung to his eyes.

"A railway wreck!" he muttered, hoarsely. "Where was it, sir? Tell me, I beseech you! And are you sure my father is dead?"

"Very sure, signore. My informant is absolutely reliable. But the details of the wreck I do not know. I am only informed of the fact of your father's death, and that his will leaves you his entire fortune."

Ferralti arose and staggered away to his room, and Uncle John watched him go pityingly, but knew no way to comfort him. When he had gone he asked gently:

"His father was an American, Duke?"

"Yes, signore."

"And wealthy, you say?"

"Exceedingly wealthy, signore."

"What was his name?"

"Ah; about that ring, my dear guest. Do you think a hundred and fifty thousand lira too much for it?"

"You said a hundred thousand."

"That was this morning, signore. The ring has increased in value since. To-morrow, without doubt, it will be worth two hundred thousand."

Tato laughed at the rueful expression on the victim's face, and, a moment after, Uncle John joined in his laughter.

"Very good, duke," he said. "I don't wish to rob you. Let us wait until to-morrow."

The brigand seemed puzzled.

"May I ask why, Signor Merreek--since you are warned?" he enquired.

"Why, it's this way, Duke. I'm just a simple, common-place American, and have lived a rather stupid existence for some time. We have no brigands at home, nor any hidden valleys or protected criminals like yourself. The romance of my surroundings interests me; your methods are unique and worth studying; if I am so rich as you think me a few extra hundred thousand lira will be a cheap price to pay for this experience. Is it not so?"

The Duke frowned.

"Do you play with me?" he asked, menacingly.

"By no means. I'm just the spectator. I expect you to make the entertainment. I'm sure it will be a good show, although the price is rather high."

Il Duca glared, but made no reply at the moment. Instead, he sat stroking Tato's hair and glowering evilly at the American.

The child whispered something in Italian, and the man nodded.

"Very well, signore," he said, more quietly. "To-morrow, then, if it so pleases you."

Then, taking Tato's hand, he slowly arose and left the veranda.

For a moment the American looked after them with a puzzled expression. Then he said to himself, with a smile: "Ah, I have solved one mystery, at any rate. Tato is a girl!"

CHAPTER XIX
A DIFFICULT POSITION

And now Uncle John, finding himself left alone, took his walkingstick and started out to explore the valley.

He felt very sorry for young Ferralti, but believed his sympathy could in no way lighten the blow caused by the abrupt news of his parent's death. He would wish to be alone with his grief for a time. By and by Mr. Merrick intended to question his fellow prisoner and try to find out something of his history.

The dale was very beautiful as it lay basking in the afternoon sun. Near the house was a large vegetable garden, which, being now shaded by the overhanging cliffs, was being tended by a sour-visaged Sicilian. Uncle John watched him for a time, but the fellow paid no heed to him. Every servant connected with the duke's establishment seemed surly and morose, and this was the more remarkable because the country folk and villagers Uncle John had met were usually merry and light-hearted.

Down by the brook were green meadows and groves of fruit trees. The little gentleman followed the stream for some distance, and finally came upon a man seated on the bank above a broad pool, intently engaged in fishing. It proved to be the dandified old doctor, who wore gloves to protect his hands and a broad-rimmed straw hat to shade his face.

Uncle John stood beside the motionless figure for a moment, watching the line. Then, forgetting he was in a foreign country, he asked carelessly:

"Any luck?"

"Not yet," was the quiet reply, in clear English. "It is too early to interest the fishes. An hour later they will bite."

"Then why did you come so soon?"

"To escape that hell-hole yonder," nodding his head toward the house.

Uncle John was surprised.

"But you are not a prisoner, doctor," he ventured to say.

"Except through the necessity of earning a livelihood. Il Duca pays well--or rather the Duchessa does, for she is the head of this household. I am skillful, and worth my price, and they know it."

"You say the Duchessa is the head of the house?"

"Assuredly, signore. Il Duca is her slave. She plans and directs everything, and her son but obeys her will."

"Did she send him to America?"

"I think so. But do not misunderstand me. The Duke is clever on his own account, and almost as wicked as his old mother. And between them they are training the child to be as bad as they are. It is dreadful."

"Have you been here long?"

"For seven years, signore."

"But you can resign whenever you please?"

"Why not? But the doubt makes me uneasy, sometimes. In another year I would like to go to Venice, and retire from professional life. I am a Venetian, you observe; no dastardly brigand of a Sicilian. And in another year I shall have sufficient means to retire and end my days in peace. Here I save every centessimo I make, for I can spend nothing."

Uncle John sat down upon the bank beside the confiding Venetian.

"Doctor," said he, "I am somewhat puzzled by this man you call Il Duca, as well as by my audacious capture and the methods employed to rob me. I'd like your advice. What shall I do?"

"The only possible thing, signore. Submit."

"Why is it the only possible thing?"

"Have you not yet discovered? Unless you pay, your friends will never hear from you again. Il Duca, by his mother's favor, is king here. He will murder you if you oppose his demands."

"Really?"

"It is quite certain, signore. He has murdered several obstinate people since I have been here, and the outside world will never know their fate. It is folly to oppose the king. Were you not rich you would not be here. Il Duca knows the exact wealth of every American who travels abroad and is likely to visit Sicily. Many escape him, but a few wander into his toils, for he is wonderfully sagacious. Mark you: he does not demand your all; he merely takes tribute, leaving his victims sufficient to render life desirable to them. If he required their all, many would as soon forfeit life as make the payment; but a tithe they will spare for the privilege of living. That is why he is so successful. And that is why he remains undisturbed. For an American, being robbed so simply, never tells of his humiliating experience. He goes home, and avoids Sicily ever after."

"H-m-m. I understand."

"But if you do not pay, you are not permitted to leave this place. You are killed at once, and the incident is over. Il Duca does not love to murder, but he takes no chances."

"I see. But suppose I pay, and then make complaint to the Italian government?"

"It has been done, signore. But the government is very blind. It does not know Il Duca d' Alcanta. Its officials are convinced he does not exist. They investigate carefully, and declare the tale is all a myth."

"Then there is no way of escape?"

"Absolutely none. Such a condition is almost inconceivable, is it not? and in this enlightened age? But it exists, and is only harmful when its victims are stubborn and rebellious. To be cheerful and pay promptly is the only sensible way out of your difficulty."

"Thank you," said Uncle John. "I shall probably pay promptly. But tell me, to satisfy my curiosity, how does your duke murder his victims?"

"He does not call it murder, as I do; he says they are suicides, or the victims of accident. They walk along a path and fall into a pit. It is deep, and they are killed. The pit is also their tomb. They are forgotten, and the trap is already set for their successors."

"Rather a gloomy picture, doctor."

"Yes. I tell you this because my nature is kind. I abhor all crime, and much prefer that you should live. But, if you die, my salario continues. I am employed to guard the health of the Duke's family--especially the old Duchessa--and have no part in this detestable business."

"Isn't that a bite?"

"No, signore. It is the current. It is not time for the fish to bite."

Uncle John arose.

"Good afternoon, doctor."

"Good afternoon, signore."

He left the old fellow sitting there and walked on. The valley was about a half mile long and from a quarter to a third of a mile in width. It resembled a huge amphitheatre in shape.

The American tramped the length of the brook, which disappeared into the rocky wall at the far end. Then he returned through the orchards to the house.

The place was silent and seemed deserted. There was a languor in the atmosphere that invited sleep. Uncle John sought his room and lay down for an afternoon nap, soon falling into a sound slumber.

When he awoke he found Ferralti seated beside his bed. The young man was pale, but composed.

"Mr. Merrick," said he, "what have you decided to do?"

Uncle John rubbed his eyes and sat up.

"I'm going to purchase that ring," he answered, "at the best price the Duke will make me."

"I am disappointed," returned Ferralti, stiffly. "I do not intend to allow myself to be robbed in this way."

"Then write a farewell letter, and I'll take it to your friends."

"It may not be necessary, sir."

Uncle John regarded him thoughtfully.

"What can you do?" he asked.

Ferralti leaned forward and whispered, softly: "I have a stout pocket-knife, with a very long blade. I shall try to kill the Duke. Once he is dead his people will not dare to oppose us, but will fly in terror. It is only Il Duca's audacity and genius that enables this robber's den to exist."

"You would rather attempt this than pay?"

"Sir, I could not bear the infamy of letting this scoundrel triumph over me."

"Well, Ferralti, you are attempting a delicate and dangerous task, but so far as I can, I will help you."

He took the revolver from his pocket and handed it to his companion.

"It's loaded in every chamber," he whispered. "Perhaps it will serve your purpose better than a knife."

Ferralti's eyes sparkled.

"Good!" he exclaimed, concealing the weapon. "I shall watch for my opportunity, so as to make no mistake. Meantime, do you bargain with the Duke, but postpone any agreement to pay."

"All right, my lad. I'll wait to see what happens. It may add a good deal to the cost of that ring, if you fail; but I'll take the chances of that for the sake of the game."

He paused a moment, and then added:

"Is your father really dead, Count?"

"Yes; the Duke has sent me the cablegram he received from his agent. I cannot doubt his authority. My father and I have not been friendly, of late years. He was a severe man, cold and unsympathetic, but I am sorry we could not have been reconciled before this awful fate overtook him. However, it is now too late for vain regrets. I tried not to disobey or antagonize my one parent, but he did not understand my nature, and perhaps I failed to understand his."

He sighed, and rising from his chair walked to the window to conceal his emotion.

Uncle John remained silent, and presently Tommaso entered to notify them that dinner would be served in a half hour, and the Duke expected them to join him at the table.

The next morning Mr. Merrick bargained pleasantly with his jailer, who seemed not averse to discussing the matter at length; but no conclusion was reached. Ferralti took no part in the conversation, but remained sullen and silent, and the Duke did not press him.

The day after, however, he insisted that he had dallied long enough, although after much argument on the part of his enforced guests he agreed to give them three days to decide, with the understanding that each day they delayed would add a goodly sum to their ransom. If at the end of the three days the Americans remained obdurate, he would invite them to take a little walk, and the affair would be terminated.

Ferralti hugged his revolver and awaited his opportunity. It seemed to Uncle John that he might have had a hundred chances to shoot the brigand, who merited no better fate than assassination at their hands; but although Ferralti was resolved upon the deed he constantly hesitated to accomplish it in cold blood, and the fact that he had three days grace induced him to put off the matter as long as possible.

He came to regret most bitterly his indecision; for something in the young man's eyes must have put the brigand on his guard. When they awoke on the third morning, which was the fifth since their imprisonment, some one had searched their rooms thoroughly. The revolver and the knife were both gone, and the loss rendered them absolutely helpless.

CHAPTER XX
UNCLE JOHN PLAYS EAVESDROPPER

It now seemed to Uncle John that further resistance to the demands of Il Duca was as useless as it was dangerous. He resented the necessity of paying a ransom as much as any man could; but imprisoned as he was in a veritable "robbers' den," without means of communicating with the authorities or the outside world, and powerless to protect his life from the vengeance of the unprincipled scoundrel who held him, the only safe and sane mode of procedure was to give in as gracefully as possible.

He formed this conclusion during a long walk around the valley, during which he once more noted the absolute seclusion of the place and the impossibility of escape by scaling the cliffs. The doctor was fishing again by the brook, but paid no heed when Uncle John tramped by. The sight of the dapper little man gave Mr. Merrick a thought, and presently he turned back and sat down beside the fisherman.

"I want to get out of this," he said, bluntly. "It was fun, at first, and rather interesting; but I've had enough of it."

The physician kept his eye on the line and made no reply.

"I want you to tell me how to escape," continued Uncle John. "It's no use saying that it can't be done, for nothing is impossible to a clever man, such as I believe you to be."

Still no reply.

"You spoke, the other day, of earning enough money to go home and live in peace for the rest of your days. Here, sir, is your opportunity to improve upon that ambition. The brigand is trying to exact a large ransom from me; I'll give it to you willingly--every penny--if you'll show me how to escape."

"Why should you do that?" enquired the doctor, still intent upon his line. "Does it matter to you who gets your money?"

"Of course," was the prompt reply. "In one case I pay it for a service rendered, and do it gladly. On the other hand, I am robbed, and that goes against the grain. Il Duca has finally decided to demand fifty thousand dollars. It shall be yours, instead, if you give me your assistance."

"Signore," said the other, calmly, "I would like this money, and I regret that it is impossible for me to earn it. But there is no means of escape from this place except by the passage through the rocks, which passage only three people know the secret of opening--Il Duca himself, the child Tato, and the old Duchessa. Perhaps Tommaso also knows; I am not certain; but he will not admit he has such knowledge. You see, signore, I am as much a prisoner as yourself."

"There ought to be some way to climb these cliffs; some secret path or underground tunnel," remarked Uncle John, musingly.

"It is more than a hundred years since this valley was made secure by a brigand ancestor of our Duchessa," was the reply. "It may be two or three centuries ago, for all I know. And ever since it has been used for just this purpose: to hold a prisoner until he was ransomed--and no such man has ever left the place alive unless he paid the price."

"Then you cannot help me?" asked Uncle John, who was weary of hearing these pessimistic declarations.

"I cannot even help myself; for I may not resign my position here unless the Duke is willing I should go."

"Good morning, doctor."

The prisoner returned slowly toward the dwelling, with its group of outhouses. By chance he found a path leading to the rear of these which he had not traversed before, and followed it until he came to a hedge of thickly set trees of some variety of cactus, which seemed to have been planted to form an enclosure. Cautiously pushing aside the branches bordering a small gap in this hedge, Uncle John discovered a charming garden lying beyond, so he quickly squeezed himself through the opening and entered.

The garden was rudely but not badly kept. There was even some attempt at ornamentation, and many of the shrubs and flowers were rare and beautiful. Narrow walks traversed the masses of foliage, and several leafy bowers invited one to escape the heat of the midday sun in their shelter. It was not a large place, and struck one as being overcrowded because so many of the plants were taller than a man's head.

Uncle John turned down one path which, after several curves and turns, came to an abrupt ending beneath the spreading branches of an acacia tree which had been converted into a bower by a thick, climbing vine, whose matted leaves and purple blossoms effectually screened off the garden beyond.

While he stood gazing around him to find a way out without retracing his steps, a clear voice within a few feet of him caused him to start. The voice spoke in vehement Italian, and came from the other side of the screen of vines. It was sharp and garrulous in tone, and although Uncle John did not understand the words he recognized their dominating accent.

The Duke replied, slowly and sullenly, and whatever he said had the effect of rousing the first speaker to fierce anger.

The American became curious. He found a place where the leaves were thinner than elsewhere, and carefully pressing them apart looked through the opening. Beyond was a clear space, well shaded and furnished with comfortable settles, tables and chairs. It adjoined a wing of the dwelling, which stood but a few paces away and was evidently occupied by the women of the household. The old Duchessa, her face still like a death mask but her eyes glittering with the brightness of a serpent's, sat enthroned within a large chair in the center of a family group. It was her sharp voice that had first aroused the American's attention. Opposite her sat the Duke, his thin face wearing an expression of gloom and dissatisfaction. The child Tato occupied a stool at her father's feet, and in the background were three serving women, sewing or embroidering. Near the Duke stood the tall brigand known as Pietro.

Answering the old woman's fierce tirade, Tato said:

"It is foolish to quarrel in Italian. The servants are listening."

"Let us then speak in English," returned the Duchessa. "These are matters the servants should not gossip about."

The Duke nodded assent. Both Tato and her grandmother spoke easily the foreign tongue; the Duke was more uncertain in his English, but understood it perfectly.

"I am still the head of this family," resumed the Duchessa, in a more moderate tone. "I insist that my will be obeyed."

"Your dignity I have the respect for," replied the Duke, laboredly; "but you grow old and foolish."

"Foolish! I?"

"Yes; you are absurd. You live in past centuries. You think to-day we must do all that your ancestors did."

"Can you do better?"

"Yes; the world has change. It has progress. With it I advance, but you do not. You would murder, rob, torture to-day as the great Duke, your grandfather, did. You think we still are of the world independent. You think we are powerful and great. Bah! we are nothing--we are as a speck of dust. But still we are the outlaws and the outcasts of Sicily, and some day Italy will crush us and we will be forgotten."

"I dare them to molest us!"

"Because you are imbecile. The world you do not know. I have travel; I see many countries; and I am wise."

"But you are still my vassal, my slave; and I alone rule here. Always have you rebelled and wanted to escape. Only my iron will has kept you here and made you do your duty."

"Since you my brother Ridolfo killed, I have little stomach for the trade of brigand. It is true. But no longer is this trade necessary. We are rich. Had I a son to inherit your business, a different thought might prevail; but I have only Tato, and a girl cannot be a successful brigand."

"Why not?" cried the old Duchessa, contemptuously. "It is the girl--always the girl--you make excuses for. But have I not ruled our domain--I, who am a woman?"

Tato herself answered, in a quiet voice.

"And what have you become, nonna, more than an outcast?" she enquired. "What use to you is money, or a power that the world would sneer at, did the world even suspect that you exist? You are a failure in life, my nonna, and I will not be like you."

The Duchessa screamed an epithet and glared at the child as if she would annihilate her; but no fitting words to reply could she find.

Uncle John smiled delightedly. He felt no sense of humiliation or revolt at eavesdropping in this den of thieves, and to be able to gain so fair a revelation of the inner life of this remarkable family was a diversion not lightly to be foregone.

"So far, we have managed to escape the law," resumed the Duke. "But always it may not be our fortune to do this, if we continue this life. It is now a good time to stop. Of one American we will gain a quarter of a million lira--a fortune--and of the other one hundred and fifty thousand lira. With what we already have it is enough and more. Quietly we will disband our men and go away. In another land we live the respectable life, in peace with all, and Tato shall be the fine lady, and forget she once was a brigand's daughter."

The child sprang up in glee, and clasping her father's neck with both arms kissed him with passionate earnestness.

Silently the Duchessa watched the scene. Her face was as pallid and immobile as ever; even the eyes seemed to have lost expression. But the next words showed that she was still unconquered.

"You shall take the money of the fat pig of an American; it is well to do so. But the youth who boldly calls himself Ferralti shall make no tribute to this family. He shall die as I have declared."

"I will not take the risk," asserted the Duke, sourly.

"Have the others who lie in the pit told tales?" she demanded.

"No; but they died alone. Here are two Americans our prisoners, and they have many and powerful friends, both at Taormina and at Naples. The man Merrick, when he goes, will tell that Ferralti is here. To obtain his person, alive or dead, the soldiers will come here and destroy us all. It is folly, and shows you are old and imbecile."

"Then go!" she cried, fiercely. "Go, you and Tato; take your money and escape. And leave me my valley, and the youth Ferralti, and my revenge. Then, if I die, if the soldiers destroy me, it is my own doing."

"In this new world, of which you know nothing, escape is not possible," replied the duke, after a moment's thought. "Ferralti must be accounted for, and because I captured him they would accuse me of his death, and even Tato might be made to suffer. No, madame. Both the Americans must be killed, or both set free for ransom."

Uncle John gave a start of dismay. Here was a development he had not expected.

"Then," said the old woman, positively, "let them both die."

"Oh, no!" exclaimed Tato. "Not that, grandmother!"

"Certainly not so," agreed the Duke. "We want their money."

"You are already rich," said the Duchessa. "You have yourself said so, and I know it is truth."

"This new world," explained the Duke, "contains of luxuries many that you have no understanding of. To be rich to-day requires more money than in your days, madre mia. With these ransoms, which already we have won, we shall have enough. Without this money my Tato would lack much that I desire for her. So of new murders I will take no risk, for the bambina's sake."

"And my revenge?"

"Bah, of what use is it? Because the boy's father married my sister Bianca, and ill-treated her, must we kill their offspring?"

"He is his father's son. The father, you say, is dead, and so also is my child Bianca. Then my hatred falls upon the son Arturo, and he must die to avenge the wrong to our race."

"More proof that you are imbecile," said the Duke, calmly. "He shall not die. He is nothing to us except a mine from whence to get gold."

"He is my grandson. I have a right to kill him."

"He is my nephew. He shall live."

"Do you defy me?"

"With certainty. I defy you. The new world permits no crazy nonna to rule a family. That is my privilege. If you persist, it is you who shall go to the pit. If you have reason, you shall remain in your garden in peace. Come, Tato; we will retire."

He arose and took the child's hand. The old woman sat staring at them in silence, but with an evil glint in her glistening eyes.

Uncle John turned around and softly made his retreat from the garden. His face wore a startled and horrified expression and on his forehead stood great beads of sweat that the sultriness of the day did not account for.

But he thought better of Il Duca.

CHAPTER XXI
THE PIT

They met an hour later at luncheon, all but the Duchessa, who sulked in her garden. Tato was bright and smiling, filled with a suppressed joy which bubbled up in spite of the little one's effort to be dignified and sedate. When her hand stole under the table to find and press that of her father, Uncle John beamed upon her approvingly; for he knew what had occurred and could sympathize with her delight.

The Duke, however, was more sombre than usual. He had defied his mother, successfully, so far; but he feared the terrible old woman more than did Tato, because he knew more of her history and of the bold and wicked deeds she had perpetrated in years gone by. Only once had a proposed victim escaped her, and that was when her own daughter Bianca had fallen in love with an American held for ransom and spirited him away from the valley through knowledge of the secret passage. It was well Bianca had fled with her lover; otherwise her mother would surely have killed her. But afterward, when the girl returned to die in the old home, all was forgiven, and only the hatred of her foreign husband, whose cruelty had driven her back to Sicily, remained to rankle in the old Duchessa's wicked heart.

No one knew her evil nature better than her son. He entertained a suspicion that he had not conquered her by his recent opposition to her will. Indeed, he would never have dared to brave her anger except for Tato's sake. Tato was his idol, and in her defense the cowardly brigand had for the moment become bold.

Tato laughed and chatted with Uncle John all through the meal, even trying at times to cheer the doleful Ferralti, who was nearly as glum and unsociable as her father. The servants and brigands at the lower end of the table looked upon the little one admiringly. It was evident she was a general favorite.

On the porch, after luncheon, the Duke broached the subject of the ransoms again, still maintaining the fable of selling his antique jewelry.

"Sir," said Uncle John, "I'm going to submit gracefully, but upon one condition."

The Duke scowled.

"I allow no conditions," he said.

"You'd better allow this one," Uncle John replied, "because it will make it easier for all of us. Of my own free will and accord I will make a present to Tato of fifty thousand dollars, and she shall have it for her dowry when she marries."

Tato clapped her hands.

"How did you know I am a girl, when I wear boys' clothes?" she asked.

Even the duke smiled, at that, but the next moment he shook his head solemnly.

"It will not do, signore," he declared, answering Uncle John's proposition. "This is a business affair altogether. You must purchase the ring, and at once."

The little American sighed. It had been his last hope.

"Very well," he said; "have your own way."

"You will send to your friends for the money?"

"Whenever you say, Duke. You've got me in a hole, and I must wiggle out the best way I can."

The brigand turned to Ferralti.

"And you, signore?" he asked.

"I do not know whether I can get the money you demand."

"But you will make the attempt, as I shall direct?"

"Yes."

"Then, signori, it is all finished. In a brief time you will leave my hospitable roof."

"The sooner the better," declared Ferralti.

They sat for a time in silence, each busy with his thoughts.

"Go to your grandmother, Tato," said the Duke, "and try to make your peace with her. If she is too angry, do not remain. To-morrow you must go into town with letters from these gentlemen to their friends."

The child kissed him and went obediently to do his will. Then the brigand spoke to Tommaso, who brought writing material from the house and placed it upon a small table.

Uncle John, without further demur, sat down to write. The Duke dictated what he should say, although he was allowed to express the words in his own characteristic style, and he followed his instructions implicitly, secretly admiring the shrewdness of the brigand's methods.

It was now Ferralti's turn. He had just seated himself at the table and taken the pen when they were startled by a shrill scream from the rear of the house. It was followed by another, and another, in quick succession.

It was Tato's voice, and the duke gave an answering cry and sprang from the veranda to dart quickly around the corner of the house. Uncle John followed him, nearly as fearful as the child's father.

Tommaso seized a short rifle that stood near and ran around the house in the other direction, when Ferralti, who for a moment had seemed dazed by the interruption, followed Tommaso rather than the others.

As they came to the rear they were amazed to see the old Duchessa, whom they had known to be feeble and dependent upon her women, rush through the garden hedge with the agility of a man, bearing in her arms the struggling form of little Tato.

The child screamed pitifully, but the woman glared upon Tommaso and Ferralti, as she passed them, with the ferocity of a tiger.

"She is mad!" cried Ferralti. "Quick, Tommaso; let us follow her."

The brigand bounded forward, with the young man scarce a pace behind him. The woman, running with wonderful speed in spite of her burden, began to ascend a narrow path leading up the face of a rugged cliff.

A yell of anguish from behind for a moment arrested Ferralti's rapid pursuit. Glancing back he saw the Duke running frantically toward them, at the same time waving his arms high above his head.

"The pit!" he shouted. "She is making for the pit. Stop her, for the love of God!"

Ferralti understood, and dashed forward again at full speed. Tommaso also understood, for his face was white and he muttered terrible oaths as he pressed on. Yet run as they might, the mad duchessa was inspired with a strength so superhuman that she kept well in advance.

But the narrow path ended half way up the cliff. It ended at a deep chasm in the rocks, the edge of which was protected by a large flat stone, like the curb of a well.

With a final leap the old woman gained this stone, and while the dreadful pit yawned at her feet she turned, and with a demoniacal laugh faced her pursuers, hugging the child close to her breast.

Tommaso and Ferralti, who were nearest, paused instinctively. It was now impossible for them to prevent the tragedy about to be enacted. The Duke, spurred on by fear, was yet twenty paces in their rear, and in a moment he also stopped, clasping his hands in a gesture of vain entreaty.

"Listen, Lugui!" his mother called to him, in a dear, high voice. "This is the child that has come between us and turned you from a man into a coward. Here alone is the cause of our troubles. Behold! I will remove it forever from our path."

With the words she lifted Tato high above her head and turned toward the pit--that terrible cleft in the rocks which was believed to have no bottom.

At her first movement Tommaso had raised his gun, and the Duke, perceiving this, called to him in an agonized voice to fire. But either the brigand wavered between his loyalty to the Duke or the Duchessa, or he feared to injure Tato, for he hesitated to obey and the moments were precious.

The child's fate hung in the balance when Ferralti snatched the weapon from the brigand's hands and fired it so hastily that he scarcely seemed to take aim.

A wild cry echoed the shot. The woman collapsed and fell, dropping Tato at her feet, where they both tottered at the edge of the pit. The child, however, clung desperately to the outer edge of the flat stone, while the Duchessa's inert form seemed to hesitate for an instant and then disappeared from view.

Tommaso ran forward and caught up the child, returning slowly along the path to place it in the father's arms. Ferralti was looking vaguely from the weapon he held to the pit, and then back again, as if not fully understanding what he had done.

"Thank you, signore," said the Duke, brokenly, "for saving my precious child."

"But I have slain your mother!" cried the young man, horrified.

"The obligation is even," replied the duke. "She was also your grandmother."

Ferralti stood motionless, his face working convulsively, his tongue refusing to utter a sound.

"But he did not shoot my grandmother at all," said Tato, who was sobbing against her father's breast; "for I heard the bullet strike the rock beside us. My grandmother's strength gave way, and she fainted. It was that that saved me, padre mia."

CHAPTER XXII
NEWS AT LAST

Kenneth Forbes had always been an unusual boy. He had grown up in an unfriendly atmosphere, unloved and uncared for, and resented this neglect with all the force of his impetuous nature. He had hated Aunt Jane, and regarded her as cruel and selfish--a fair estimate of her character--until Aunt Jane's nieces taught him to be more considerate and forgiving. Patricia, especially, had exercised a gentler influence upon the arbitrary youth, and as a consequence they had become staunch friends.

When the unexpected inheritance of a fortune changed the boy's condition from one of dependence to one of importance he found he had no longer any wrongs to resent; therefore his surly and brusque moods gradually disappeared, and he became a pleasant companion to those he cared for. With strangers he still remained reserved and suspicious, and occasionally the old sullen fits would seize him and it was well to avoid his society while they lasted.

On his arrival at Taormina, Kenneth had entered earnestly into the search for Uncle John, whom he regarded most affectionately; and, having passed the day tramping over the mountains, he would fill the evening with discussions and arguments with the nieces concerning the fate of their missing uncle.

But as the days dragged wearily away the search slackened and was finally abandoned. Kenneth set up his easel in the garden and began to paint old Etna, with its wreath of snow and the soft gray cloud of vapor that perpetually hovered over it.

"Anyone with half a soul could paint that!" said Patsy; and as a proof of her assertion the boy did very well indeed, except that his uneasiness on Mr. Merrick's account served to distract him more or less.

Nor was Kenneth the only uneasy one. Mr. Watson, hard-headed man of resource as he was, grew more and more dejected as he realized the impossibility of interesting the authorities in the case. The Sicilian officials were silent and uncommunicative; the Italians wholly indifferent. If strangers came to Taormina and got into difficulties, the government was in no way to blame. It was their duty to tolerate tourists, but those all too energetic foreigners must take care of themselves.

Probably Mr. Watson would have cabled the State Department at Washington for assistance had he not expected each day to put him in communication with his friend, and in the end he congratulated himself upon his patience. The close of the week brought a sudden and startling change in the situation.

The girls sat on the shaded terrace one afternoon, watching the picture of Etna grow under Kenneth's deft touches, when they observed a child approaching them with shy diffidence. It was a beautiful Sicilian boy, with wonderful brown eyes and a delicate profile. After assuring himself that the party of young Americans was quite separate from any straggling guest of the hotel, the child came near enough to say, in a low tone:

"I have a message from Signor Merrick."

They crowded around him eagerly then, raining questions from every side; but the boy shrank away and said, warningly:

"If we are overheard, signorini mia, it will be very bad. No one must suspect that I am here."

"Is my uncle well?" asked Patsy, imploringly.

"Quite well, mees."

"And have you also news of Count Ferralti?" anxiously enquired Louise.

"Oh, Ferralti? He is better. Some teeth are knocked out, but he eats very well without them," replied the child, with an amused laugh.

"Where are our friends, my lad?" Kenneth asked.

"I cannot describe the place, signore; but here are letters to explain all." The child produced a bulky package, and after a glance at each, in turn, placed it in Patsy's hands. "Read very secretly, signorini, and decide your course of action. To-morrow I will come for your answer. In the meantime, confide in no one but yourselves. If you are indiscreet, you alone will become the murderers of Signor Merrick and the sad young Ferralti."

"Who are you?" asked Beth, examining the child closely.

"I am called Tato, signorina mia."

"Where do you live?"

"It is all explained in the letters, believe me."

Beth glanced at Patricia, who was examining the package, and now all crowded around for a glimpse of Uncle John's well-known handwriting. The wrapper was inscribed:

"To Miss Doyle, Miss De Graf and Miss Merrick, Hotel Castello-a-Mare, Taormina. By the safe hands of Tato."

Inside were two letters, one addressed to Louise personally. She seized this and ran a little distance away, while Beth took Uncle John's letter from Patsy's trembling hands, and having opened it read aloud in a clear and composed voice the following:

"My dear Nieces: (and also my dear friends, Silas Watson and Kenneth Forbes, if they are with you) Greeting! You have perhaps been wondering at my absence, which I will explain by saying that I am visiting a noble acquaintance in a very cozy and comfortable retreat which I am sure would look better from a distance. My spirits and health are A No. 1 and it is my intention to return to you as soon as you have executed a little commission for me, which I want you to do exactly as I hereby instruct you. In other words, if you don't execute the commission you will probably execute me.

"I have decided to purchase a valuable antique ring from my host, at a price of fifty thousand dollars, which trifling sum I must have at once to complete the transaction, for until full payment is made I cannot rejoin you. Therefore you must hasten to raise the dough. Here's the programme, my dear girls: One of you must go by first train to Messina and cable Isham, Marvin & Co. to deposit with the New York correspondents of the Banca Commerciale Italiana fifty thousand dollars, and have instructions cabled to the Messina branch of that bank to pay the sum to the written order of John Merrick. This should all be accomplished within twenty-four hours. Present the enclosed order, together with my letter of credit and passport, which will identify my signature, and draw the money in cash. Return with it to Taormina and give it secretly to the boy Tato, who will bring it to me. I will rejoin you within three hours after I have paid for the ring.

"This may seem a strange proceeding to you, my dears, but you must not hesitate to accomplish it--if you love me. Should my old friend Silas Watson be now with you, as I expect him to be, he will assist you to do my bidding, for he will be able to realize, better than I can now explain, how important it is to me.

"Also I beg you to do a like service for Count Ferralti, who is entrusting his personal commission, to Louise. He also must conclude an important purchase before he can return to Taormina.

"More than this I am not permitted to say in this letter. Confide in no stranger, or official of any sort, and act as secretly and quietly as possible. I hope soon to be with you.

"Very affectionately, UNCLE JOHN."

"What does it all mean?" asked Patsy, bewildered, when Beth had finished reading.

"Why, it is clear enough, I'm sure," said Kenneth. "Uncle John is imprisoned by brigands, and the money he requires is his ransom. We must get it as soon as possible, you know, and luckily he is so rich that he won't miss this little draft at all."

Beth sat silent, angrily staring at the letter.

"I suppose," said Patsy, hesitating, "the robbers will do the dear uncle some mischief, if he doesn't pay."

"Just knock him on the head, that's all," said the boy. "But there's no need to worry. We can get the money easily."

Suddenly Beth jumped up.

"Where's that girl?" she demanded, sharply.

"What girl?"

"Tato."

"Tato, my dear coz, is a boy," answered Kenneth; "and he disappeared ages ago."

"You must be blind," said Beth, scornfully, "not to recognize a girl when you see one. A boy, indeed!"

"Why, he dressed like a boy," replied Kenneth, hesitatingly.

"So much the more disgraceful," sniffed Beth. "She belongs to those brigands, I suppose."

"Looks something like Victor Valdi," said Patsy, thoughtfully.

"Il Duca? Of course! I see it myself, now. Patricia, it is that wicked duke who has captured Uncle John."

"I had guessed that," declared Patsy, smiling.

"He must be a handsome rascal," observed Kenneth, "for the child is pretty as a picture."

"He isn't handsome at all," replied Beth; "but there is a look about the child's eyes that reminds me of him."

"That's it, exactly," agreed Patsy.

Louise now approached them with a white, frightened face.

"Isn't it dreadful!" she moaned. "They are going to kill Ferralti unless he gives them thirty thousand dollars."

"And I don't believe he can raise thirty cents," said Patsy, calmly.

"Oh, yes, he can," answered Louise, beginning to cry. "Hi--his--father is d--dead, and has left him--a--fortune."

"Don't blubber, Lou," said the boy, chidingly; "in that case your dago friend is as well off as need be. But I suppose you're afraid the no-account Count won't figure his life is worth thirty thousand dollars. It does seem like an awful price to pay for a foreigner."

"It isn't that," said Louise, striving to control her emotion. "He says he hates to be robbed. He wouldn't pay a penny if he could help it."

"Good for the Count! I don't blame him a bit," exclaimed Beth. "It is a beastly shame that free born Americans should be enslaved by a crew of thieving Sicilians, and obliged to purchase their freedom!"

"True for you," said Kenneth, nodding. "But what are we going to do about it?"

"Pay, of course," decided Patsy, promptly. "Our Uncle John is too precious to be sacrificed for all the money in the world. Come; let's go and find Mr. Watson. We ought not to lose a moment's time."

The lawyer read Uncle John's letter carefully, as well as the one from Count Ferralti, which Louise confided to him with the request that he keep the young man's identity a secret for a time, until he could reveal it to her cousins in person.

"The only thing to be done," announced Mr. Watson, "is to carry out these instructions faithfully. We can send the cable messages from here, and in the morning Louise and I will take the train for Messina and remain there until we get the money."

"It's an outrage!" cried Beth.

"Of course, my dear. But it can't be helped. And your uncle is wise to take the matter so cheerfully. After all, it is little enough to pay for one's life and liberty, and our friend is so wealthy that he will never feel the loss at all."

"It isn't that; it's the principle of the thing that I object to," said the girl. "It's downright disgraceful to be robbed so easily."

"To be sure; but the disgrace is Italy's, not ours. Object all you want to, Beth, dear," continued the old lawyer, smiling at her; "but nevertheless we'll pay as soon as possible, and have done with it. What we want now is your Uncle John, and we want him mighty badly."

"Really, the pirates didn't charge enough for him," added Patsy.

So Mr. Watson sent the cables to John Merrick's bankers and Count Ferralti's attorney, and the next morning went with Louise to Messina.

Frascatti drove all the party down the road to the station at Giardini, and as the train pulled out, Beth, who had remained seated in the victoria with Patricia and Kenneth, suddenly stood up to pull the vetturino's sleeve.

"Tell me, Frascatti," she whispered, "isn't that Il Duca's child? Look--that little one standing in the corner?"

"Why, yes; it is really Tato," answered the man, before he thought to deny it.

"Very well; you may now drive us home," returned Beth, a shade of triumph in her voice.

CHAPTER XXIII
BETH BEGINS TO PLOT

Once back in their sitting-room behind closed doors, Beth, Patsy and Kenneth got their three heads together and began eagerly to discuss a plot which Beth had hinted of on the way home and now unfolded in detail. And while they still whispered together a knock at the door startled them and made them look rather guilty until the boy answered the call and admitted little Tato.

The child's beautiful face wore a smile of demure satisfaction as Tato bowed respectfully to the young Americans.

Kenneth winked at Beth from behind the visitor's back.

"As you have a guest," he remarked, with a yawn that was somewhat rude, "I shall now go and take my nap."

"What, do you sleep so early in the day, you lazy-bones?" asked Patsy, brightly.

"Any time, my dear, is good enough for an overworked artist," he replied. "Au revoir, my cousins. See you at luncheon."

With this he strolled away, and when he had gone Beth said to Tato:

"Won't you sit down, signorina?"

"Do you mean me?" asked the child, as if surprised.

"Yes; I can see plainly that you are a girl."

"And a pretty one, too, my dear," added Patsy.

Tato blushed as if embarrassed, but in a moment smiled upon the American girls.

"Do you think me immodest, then?" she asked, anxiously.

"By no means, my dear," Beth assured her. "I suppose you have an excellent reason for wearing boys' clothes."

"So I have, signorina. I live in the mountains, where dresses catch in the crags, and bother a girl. And my father has always been heart-broken because he had no son, and likes to see me in this attire. He has many errands for me, too, where a boy may go unnoticed, yet a girl would attract too much attention. This is one of the errands, signorini. But now tell me, if you please, how have you decided to answer the letters of Signor Merrick and Signor Ferralti?"

"Oh, there was but one way to answer them, Tato," replied Beth, composedly. "We have sent Mr. Watson and our cousin Louise Merrick to Messina to get the money. If our friends in America act promptly Mr. Watson and Louise will return by to-morrow afternoon's train, and be prepared to make the payment."

"That is well, signorina," responded Tato.

"We are to give the money to you, I suppose?" said Patsy.

"Yes; I will return for it to-morrow afternoon," answered the child, with business-like gravity. Then she looked earnestly from one to the other of the two girls. "You must act discreetly, in the meantime, you know. You must not talk to anyone, or do anything to imperil your uncle's safety."

"Of course not, Tato."

"I beg you not, signorini. The uncle is a good man, and brave. I do not wish him to be injured."

"Nor do we, Tato."

"And the young man is not a coward, either. He has been kind to me. But he is sad, and not so pleasant to talk with as the uncle."

"True enough, Tato," said Beth.

Patsy had been examining the child with curious intentness. The little one was so lovely and graceful, and her voice sounded so soft and womanly, that Patsy longed to take her in her arms and hug her.

"How old are you, dear?" she asked.

Tato saw the friendly look, and answered with a smile.

"Perhaps as old as you, signorina, although I am so much smaller. I shall be fifteen in a month."

"So old!"

Tato laughed merrily.

"Ah, you might well say 'so young,' amico mia! To be grown up is much nicer; do you not think so? And then I shall not look such a baby as now, and have people scold me when I get in the way, as they do little bambini."

"But when you are grown you cannot wear boys' clothing, either."

Tato sighed.

"We have a saying in Sicily that 'each year has its sunshine and rain,' which means its sorrow and its joy," she answered. "Perhaps I sometimes think more of the tears than of the laughter, although I know that is wrong. Not always shall I be a mountaineer, and then the soft dresses of the young girls shall be my portion. Will I like them better? I do not know. But I must go now, instead of chattering here. Farewell, signorini, until to-morrow."

"Will you not remain with us?"

"Oh, no; although you are kind. I am expected home. But to-morrow I will come for the money. You will be silent?"

"Surely, Tato."

The child smiled upon them pleasantly. It was a relief to deal with two tender girls instead of cold and resentful men, such as she had sometimes met. At the door she blew a kiss to them, and darted away.

In the courtyard Frascatti saw her gliding out and discreetly turned his head the other way.

Tato took the old road, circling around the theatre and through the narrow, winding streets of the lower town to the Catania Gate. She looked back one or twice, but no one noticed her. If any of the villagers saw her approaching they slipped out of her path.

Once on the highway, however, Tato became lost in reflection. Her mission being successfully accomplished, it required no further thought; but the sweet young American girls had made a strong impression upon the lonely Sicilian maid, and she dreamed of their pretty gowns and ribbons, their fresh and comely faces, and the gentleness of their demeanor.

Tato was not gentle. She was wild and free and boyish, and had no pretty gowns whatever. But what then? She must help her father to get his fortune, and then he had promised her that some day they would go to Paris or Cairo and live in the world, and be brigands no longer.

She would like that, she thought, as she clambered up the steep paths; and perhaps she would meet these American girls again, or others like them, and make them her friends. She had never known a girl friend, as yet.

These ambitions would yesterday have seemed far in the dim future; but now that her stern old grandmother was gone it was possible her father would soon fulfill his promises. While the Duchessa lived she ruled them all, and she was a brigand to the backbone. Now her father's will prevailed, and he could refuse his child nothing.

Kenneth was not an expert detective, but he had managed to keep Tato in sight without being suspected by her. He had concealed himself near the Catania Gate, through which he knew she must pass, and by good luck she had never looked around once, so intent were her musings.

When she came to the end of the path and leaned against the rock to sing the broken refrain which was the "open sesame" to the valley, the boy was hidden snug behind a boulder where he could watch her every movement.

Then the rock opened; Tato passed in, and the opening closed behind her.

Kenneth found a foothold and climbed up the wall of rock, higher and higher, until at last he crept upon a high ridge and looked over.

The hidden valley lay spread before him in all its beauty, but the precipice at his feet formed a sheer drop of a hundred feet or more, and he drew back with a shudder.

Then he took courage to look again, and observed the house, on the porch of which stood Tato engaged in earnest conversation with a tall, dark Sicilian. Uncle John was nowhere to be seen, but the boy understood that he was there, nevertheless, and realized that his prison was so secure that escape was impossible.

And now he climbed down again, a much more difficult feat than getting up. But although he was forced to risk his life several times, he was agile and clear-headed, and finally dropped to the path that led to the secret door of the passage.

His next thought was to mark the exact location of the place, so that he could find it again; and as he returned slowly along the paths through the rocky fissures he took mental note of every curve and communication, and believed he could now find his way to the retreat of the brigands at any time he chose.

CHAPTER XXIV
PATSY'S NEW FRIEND

"I must say that I don't like the job," said Patsy, the next morning, as she stood by the window and faced Beth and Kenneth. "Suppose we fail?"

"In the bright lexicon of youth--"

"Shut up, Ken. If we fail," said Beth, "we will be no worse off than before."

"And if we win," added the boy, "they'll think twice before they try to rob Americans again."

"Well, I'm with you, anyhow," declared Patricia. "I can see it's risky, all right; but as you say, no great harm will be done if we slip up."

"You," announced Beth, gravely, "must be the captain."

"It isn't in me, dear. You figured the thing out, and Ken and I will follow your lead."

"No," said Beth, decidedly; "I'm not quick enough, either in thought or action, to be a leader, Patsy. And there's a bit of deception required that I couldn't manage. That clever little thing, Tato, would know at once I was up to some mischief; but she would never suspect you."

"I like that compliment," replied Patricia. "I may deserve it, of course; but it strikes me Louise is the one best fitted for such work."

"We can't let Louise into this plot," said the boy, positively; "she'd spoil it all."

"Don't be silly, Patsy," said Beth. "You're genuine and frank, and the child likes you. I could see that yesterday. All you have to do is to be nice to her and win her confidence; and then, when the climax comes, you must be the spokesman and talk straight out from the shoulder. You can do that all right."

"I'll bet on her," cried Kenneth, with an admiring look at the girl.

"Then," said Patsy, "it is all arranged, and I'm the captain. And is it agreed that we won't lisp a word to Mr. Watson or Louise?"

"Not a word."

"Here," said Kenneth, drawing a revolver from his pocket, "is Uncle John's pop-gun. It's the only one I could find in his room, so he must have taken the other with him. Be careful of it, Patsy, for it's loaded all 'round. Can you shoot?"

"No; but I suppose the pistol can. I know enough to pull the trigger."

"And when you do, remember to point it away from your friends. Now hide it, my dear, and be careful of it."

Patsy concealed the weapon in the bosom of her dress, not without making a wry face and shivering a bit.

"Have you got your revolver, Beth?" asked the boy.

"Yes."

"And she can shoot just wonderfully!" exclaimed Patsy. "Yesterday she picked an orange off a tree with a bullet. You should have seen her."

"I know," said Ken, nodding. "I've seen Beth shoot before, and she's our main reliance in this conspiracy. For my part, I can hit a mark sometimes, and sometimes I can't. See here." He exhibited a beautiful pearl and silver-mounted weapon which he drew from his pocket. "Mr. Watson and I have carried revolvers ever since we came to Sicily, but we've never had occasion to use them. I can hardly believe, even now, that this beautiful place harbors brigands. It's such a romantic incident in our prosaic world of to-day. And now, young ladies, we are armed to the teeth and can defy an army. Eh, Captain Pat?"

"If you're not more respectful," said the girl, "I'll have you court-marshalled and drummed out of camp."

On the afternoon train came Louise and Mr. Watson from Messina. The American agents had responded promptly, and the bank had honored the orders and delivered the money without delay.

"It is all safe in my satchel," said the lawyer, as they rode together to the hotel; "and our dear friends are as good as rescued already. It's pretty bulky, Kenneth--four hundred thousand lira--but it is all in notes on the Banca d'Italia, for we couldn't manage gold."

"Quite a haul for the brigand," observed Kenneth, thoughtfully.

"True; but little enough for the lives of two men. That is the way I look at the transaction. And, since our friends can afford the loss, we must be as cheerful over the thing as possible. It might have been a tragedy, you know."

Louise shivered.

"I'm glad it is all over," she said, gratefully.

The conspirators looked at one another and smiled, but held their peace.

Arriving at the hotel, Beth and Kenneth at once disappeared, saying they were going to town, as they would not be needed longer. Patsy accompanied their cousin and the lawyer to the sitting-room, where presently Tato came to them.

"Well, little one," said the lawyer, pleasantly, "We have secured the money required to enable Mr. Merrick to purchase the ring, and Mr.--er--Count Ferralti to buy his bracelet. Will you count it?"

"Yes, signore, if you please," replied Tato, with a sober face.

Mr. Watson drew out two packages of bank notes and placed them upon the table. The child, realizing the importance of the occasion, carefully counted each bundle, and then replaced the wrappers.

"The amounts are correct, signore," she said. "I thank you for making my task so easy. And now I will go."

The lawyer brought a newspaper and wrapped the money in it once again.

"It is always dangerous to carry so much money," said he; "but now no one will be likely to suspect the contents of your package."

Tato smiled.

"No one would care to molest me," she said; "for they fear those that protect me. Good afternoon, signore. Your friends will be with you in time to dine in your company. Good afternoon, signorini," turning to Patsy and Louise.

"I'll walk a little way with you; may I?" asked Patsy, smiling into Tato's splendid eyes.

"To be sure, signorina," was the quick response.

Patricia caught up a sunshade and followed the child out at the side entrance, which was little used. Tato took the way along the old road, and Patsy walked beside her, chatting brightly of the catacombs, the Norman villa that showed its checkered tower above the trees and the ancient wall that still hemmed in the little village.

"I love Taormina," she said, earnestly, "and shall be sorry to leave it. You must be very happy, Tato, to be able to live here always."

"It is my birthplace," she said; "but I long to get away from it and see other countries. The view is fine, they say; but it tires me. The air is sweet and pure; but it oppresses me. The climate is glorious; but I have had enough of it. In other places there is novelty, and many things that Sicily knows nothing of."

"That is true," replied Patsy, tucking the little one's arm underneath her own, with a sympathetic gesture. "I know just how you feel, Tato. You must come to America some day, and visit me. I will make you very welcome, dear, and you shall be my friend."

The child looked into her face earnestly.

"You do not hate me, signorina, because--because--"

"Because why?"

"Because my errand to you has been so lawless and--and--unfriendly?"

"Ah, Tato, you do not choose this life, do you?"

"No, signorina."

"It is forced on you by circumstances, is it not?"

"Truly, signorina."

"I know. You would not long so wistfully to change your condition if you enjoyed being a little brigand. But nothing that has passed must interfere with our friendship, dear. If I were in your place, you see, I would do just as you have done. It is not a very honest life, Tato, nor one to be proud of; but I'm not going to blame you one bit."

They had passed the Catania Gate and reached the foot of one of the mountain paths. Tato paused, hesitatingly.

"Oh, I'll go a little farther," said Patsy, promptly. "No one will notice two girls, you know. Shall I carry your parcel for a time?"

"No," replied the child, hugging it close with her disengaged arm. But she offered no objection when Patsy continued to walk by her side.

"Have you any brothers or sisters, Tato?"

"No, signorina."

"Have you a mother?"

"No, signorina. My father and I are alone."

"I know him well, Tato. We were on the ship together, crossing the ocean. He was gruff and disagreeable, but I made him talk to me and smile."

"I know; he has told me of the Signorina Patsy. He is fond of you."

"Yet he robbed my uncle."

The child flushed, and drew away her arm.

"That is it. That is why you should hate me," she replied, bitterly. "I know it is robbery, and brigandage, although my father masks it by saying he sells antiques. Until now I have seen nothing wrong in this life, signorina; but you have made me ashamed."

"Why, dear?"

"Because you are so good and gentle, and so forgiving."

Patsy laughed.

"In reality, Tato, I am resentful and unforgiving. You will find out, soon, that I am a very human girl, and then I will not make you ashamed. But your father's business is shameful, nevertheless."

Tato was plainly puzzled, and knew not what to reply. But just then they reached the end of the crevasse, and the child said:

"You must return now, Signorina Patsy."

"But why cannot I go on with you, and come back with my uncle?"

Tato hesitated. Accustomed as she was to duplicity and acting, in her capacity as lure for her thieving father, the child was just now softened by Patsy's kindly manner and the successful accomplishment of her mission. She had no thought of any treachery or deception on the part of the American girl, and the request seemed to her natural enough.

"If you like," she decided, "you may come as far as the barrier, and there wait for your uncle. It will not be long."

"Very well, dear."

Tato clambered over the dividing rock and dropped into the path beyond. Patsy sprang lightly after her. A short distance farther and they reached the barrier.

"This is the place, signorina. You will sit upon that stone, and wait until your uncle appears." She hesitated, and then added, softly: "I may not see you again. But you will not forget me?"

"Never, Tato. And if you come to America you must not forget to visit me. Remember, whatever happens, that we are friends, and must always remain so."

The child nodded, gratefully. Then, leaning against the face of the cliff, she raised her voice and warbled clearly the bit of song that served as the signal to her father.

CHAPTER XXV
TURNING THE TABLES

No sooner had the notes ceased than Kenneth sprang from behind a rock that had concealed him and grasped the child in his strong arms, trying to cover her mouth at the same time to prevent her from crying out.

Tato developed surprising strength. The adventure of yesterday had so thoroughly frightened her that when she found herself again seized she struggled madly. The boy found that he could scarcely hold her, so he enfolded her in both his arms and, letting her scream as she might, picked up her tiny form and mounted the slope of the hill, leaping from rock to rock until he came to a broad boulder twenty feet or more above the path. Here he paused, panting, and awaited results.

The rock doors had opened promptly. Even while Kenneth struggled with the brigand's daughter Patsy could see straight through the tunnel and into the valley beyond. The child had dropped her bundle in the effort to escape, and while Kenneth was leaping with her up the crags Patsy ran forward and secured the money, returning quickly to her position facing the tunnel.

And now they heard shouts and the sound of hastening feet as Il Duca ran from the tunnel, followed closely by two of his brigands. They paused a moment at the entrance, as if bewildered, but when the father saw his child in the grasp of a stranger and heard her screams he answered with a roar of fury and prepared to scramble up the rock to rescue her.

That was where Patsy showed her mettle. She hastily covered the brigand with her revolver and shouted warningly:

"Stop, or you are a dead man!"

It was wonderfully dramatic and effective.

Il Duca shrank back, scowling, for he had no weapon at hand. Leaning against the entrance to his valley he glared around to determine the number of his foes and the probable chance of defeating them.

Kenneth laughed boyishly at his discomfiture. Kneeling down, the youth grasped Tato by both wrists and lowered her body over the edge of the rock so that her feet just touched a little ledge beneath. He continued to hold fast to her wrists, though, and there she remained, stretched against the face of the rock fronting the path, in full view of all, but still unable to move.

From this exasperating sight Il Duca glanced at Patsy. She was holding the revolver rigidly extended, and her blue eyes blazed with the excitement of the moment. It was a wonder she did not pull the trigger inadvertently, and the thought that she might do so caused the brigand to shudder.

Turning half around he beheld a third enemy quietly seated upon the rocks directly across the path from Kenneth, her pose unconcerned as she rested her chin lightly upon her left hand. It was Beth, who held her revolver nonchalantly and gazed upon the scene below her with calm interest.

The Duke gave a cough to clear his throat. His men hung back of him, silent and motionless, for they did not like this absolute and dangerous defiance of their chief.

"Tell me, then, Tato," he called in English, "what is the cause of this trouble?"

"I do not know, my father, except that these are friends of Signor Merrick who have secretly followed me here."

The carefully arranged programme gave Patsy a speech at this point, but she had entirely forgotten it.

"Let me explain," said Beth, coldly. "You have dared to detain in your robbers' den the persons of Mr. Merrick and Count Ferralti. You have also demanded a ransom for their release. That is brigandage, which is denounced by the laws of Sicily. We have appealed to the authorities, but they are helpless to assist us. Therefore, being Americans, we have decided to assist ourselves. We command you to deliver to us on this spot, safe and uninjured, the persons of our friends, and that without any unnecessary delay."

The Duke listened with a sneer.

"And if we refuse, signorina?"

"If you refuse--if you do not obey at once--I swear that I will shoot your child, Tato, whose body yonder awaits my bullet. And afterward I shall kill you."

As she spoke she levelled the revolver and aimed it carefully at the exposed body of the child.

The brigand paled, and grasped the rock to steady himself.

"Bah! No girl can shoot from that distance," he exclaimed, scornfully.

"Indeed! Take care of your finger," called Beth, and a shot echoed sharply along the mountain side.

The brigand jumped and uttered a yell, at the same time whipping his right hand underneath his left arm; for Beth's bullet had struck one of his fingers and then flattened itself against the cliff.

That settled all argument, as far as Il Duca was concerned; for he now had ample evidence that the stern-eyed girl above him could shoot, and was not to be trifled with. All his life he had ruled by the terror of his threats; today he was suddenly vanquished by a determination he dared not withstand.

"Enough!" he cried. "Have your way."

He spoke to his men in Italian, and they hastened through the tunnel, glad to escape.

Following their departure there was a brief silence, during which all stood alert. Then, Tato, still half suspended against the cliff, said in a clear, soft voice:

"Father, if you think you can escape, let them shoot me, and keep your prisoners. The money for their ransom I brought to this place, and they will pay it even yet to save their friends from your vengeance. Do not let these wild Americans defeat us, I beg of you. I am not afraid. Save yourself, and let them shoot me, if they will!"

Kenneth afterward declared that he thought "the jig was up" then, for they had no intention whatever of harming Tato. It was all merely a bit of American "bluff," and it succeeded because the brigand was a coward, and dared not emulate his daughter's courage.

"No, no, Tato!" cried the Duke, brokenly, as he wrung his hands in anguish. "There is more money to be had, but I have only one child. They shall not harm a hair of your head, my pretty one!"

Patsy wanted to yell "bravo!" but wisely refrained. Her eyes were full of tears, though, and her resolution at ebb tide.

Fortunately the men had made haste. They returned with surprising promptness, pushing the amazed prisoners before them.

Uncle John, as he emerged from the tunnel, looked around upon the tragic scene and gasped:

"Well, I declare!"

Count Ferralti was more composed, if equally surprised. He lifted his hat politely to Beth and Patsy, and smiled with great satisfaction.

"You are free," said Il Duca, harshly. "Go!"

They lost no time in getting the brigands between themselves and the mouth of the tunnel, and then Kenneth gently drew Tato to a place beside him and assisted her to clamber down the path.

"Good bye, little one," he said, pleasantly; "you're what we call a 'brick' in our country. I like you, and I'm proud of you."

Tato did not reply. With streaming eyes she was examining her father's shattered hand, and sobbing at sight of the blood that dripped upon the rocks at his feet.

"Get inside!" called Beth, sharply; "and close up that rock. Lively, now!"

The "girl who could shoot" still sat toying with her revolver, and the mountaineers obeyed her injunction. The rock promptly closed, and the group of Americans was left alone.

Then Beth came slowly down to where Patsy was hugging Uncle John in a wild frenzy of delight, and Count Ferralti was shaking Kenneth's hand with a face eloquent of emotion.

"Come," said she, her voice sounding faint and weary, "let us get away from here. It was a pretty game, while it lasted, but I'll feel safer when we are home again. Where's the money?"

"I've got it," said Kenneth, holding up the package.

"What! didn't you pay?" demanded Uncle John, astounded.

"Of course not, dear," said Patsy, gleefully. "Did you think your nieces would let you be robbed by a bunch of dagoes?"

Ferralti caught hold of Beth's swaying form.

"Look after your cousin," he said, sharply. "I think she has fainted!"

CHAPTER XXVI
THE COUNT UNMASKS

"And now," said Uncle John, as he sat in their cosy sitting-room, propped in an easy chair with his feet upon a stool, "it's about time for you to give an account of yourselves, you young rascals."

They had eaten a late but very satisfactory dinner at the Castello-a-Mare, where the return of the missing ones was hailed with joy by the proprietor and his assistants. Even the little bewhiskered head-waiter, who resembled a jack-in-the-box more than he did a man, strove to celebrate the occasion by putting every good thing the house afforded before the returned guests. For, although they dared not interfere to protect the victims of the terrible Il Duca, the hotel people fully recognized the fact that brigandage was not a good advertisement for Taormina, and hoped the "little incident" would not become generally known.

Old Silas Watson, dignified lawyer as he was, actually danced a hornpipe when he beheld his old friend safe and sound. But he shook his head reproachfully when he learned of the adventure his ward and the two girls had undertaken with such temerity but marvelous success.

Beth had quickly recovered from her weakness, although Kenneth had insisted on keeping her arm all the way home. But the girl had been silent and thoughtful, and would eat nothing at dinner.

When they had gathered in their room to talk it all over the lawyer thought his young friends deserved a reproof.

"The money wasn't worth the risk, you crazy lunatics!" he said.

"It wasn't the money at all," replied Patsy, demurely.

"No?"

"It was the principle of the thing. And wasn't Beth just wonderful, though?"

"Shucks!" said Kenneth. "She had to go and faint, like a ninny, and she cried all the way home, because she had hurt the brigand's finger."

The girl's eyes were still red, but she answered the boy's scornful remark by saying, gravely:

"I am sorry it had to be done. I'll never touch a revolver again as long as I live."

Uncle John gathered his brave niece into an ample embrace.

"I'm very proud of you, my dear," he said, stroking her hair lovingly, "and you mustn't pay any attention to that silly boy. I've always known you were true blue, Beth, and now you have proved it to everyone. It may have been a reckless thing to do, as Mr. Watson says, but you did it like a major, and saved our self-esteem as well as our money."

"Hurrah for Beth!" yelled the boy, changing his colors without a blush.

"If you don't shut up, I'll box your ears," said his guardian, sternly.

Uncle John and young Ferralti were the heroes of the evening. The little old gentleman smoked a big cigar and beamed upon his nieces and friends with intense satisfaction, while Ferralti sat glum and silent beside Louise until an abrupt challenge from Mr. Merrick effectually aroused him.

"I've only one fault to find with this young man," was the observation referred to: "that he made our acquaintance under false pretenses. When a fairly decent fellow becomes an impostor there is usually reason for it, and I would like Count Ferralti--or whatever his name is--to give us that reason and make a clean breast of his deception."

Ferralti bowed, with a serious face, but looked significantly toward the other members of the company.

"Whatever you have to say should be heard by all," declared Uncle John, answering the look.

"Perhaps you are right, Mr. Merrick, and all present are entitled to an explanation," answered the young man, slowly. "I may have been foolish, but I believe I have done nothing that I need be ashamed of. Fortunately, there is now no further reason for concealment on my part, and in listening to my explanation I hope you will be as considerate as possible."

They were attentive enough, by this time, and every eye was turned, not unkindly, upon the youth who had so long been an enigma to them all--except, perhaps, to Louise.

"I am an American by birth, and my name is Arthur Weldon."

In the pause that followed Uncle John gave a soft whistle and Patsy laughed outright, to the undisguised indignation of Louise.

"Years ago," resumed the youth, "my father, who was a rich man, made a trip to Sicily and, although I did not know this until recently, was seized by brigands and imprisoned in the hidden valley we have just left. There he fell in love with a beautiful girl who was the daughter of the female brigand known as the Duchess of Alcanta, and who assisted him to escape and then married him. It was a pretty romance at the time, but when my father had taken his bride home to New York and became immersed in the details of his business, his love grew cold and he began to neglect his wife cruelly. He became a railway president and amassed a great fortune, but was not so successful a husband as he was a financier. The result was that the Sicilian girl, after some years of unhappiness and suffering, deserted him and returned to her own country, leaving her child, then three years old, behind her. To be frank with you, it was said at the time that my mother's mind had become unbalanced, or she would not have abandoned me to the care of a loveless father, but I prefer to think that she had come to hate her husband so bitterly that she could have no love for his child or else she feared that her terrible mother would kill me if I came into her power. Her flight mattered little to my father, except that it made him more stern and tyrannical toward me. He saw me very seldom and confided my education to servants. So I grew up practically unloved and uncared for, and when the proper time arrived I was sent to college. My father now gave me an ample allowance, and at the close of my college career called me into his office and ordered me to enter the employ of the railway company. I objected to this. I did not like the business and had other plans for my future. But he was stubborn and dictatorial, and when I continued unsubmissive he threatened to cast me off entirely and leave his fortune to charity, since he had no other near relatives. He must have thought better of this decision afterward, for he gave me a year to decide whether or not I would obey him. At the end of that time, he declared, I would become either a pauper or his heir, at my option.

"It was during this year that I formed the acquaintance of your niece, Miss Merrick, and grew to love her devotedly. Louise returned my affection, but her mother, learning of my quarrel with my father, refused to sanction our engagement until I was acknowledged his heir. I was forbidden her house, but naturally we met elsewhere, and when I knew she was going to Europe with you, sir, who had never seen me, we hit upon what we thought was a happy and innocent plan to avoid the long separation. I decided to go to Europe also, and without you or your other nieces suspecting, my identity, attach myself to your party and enjoy the society of Louise while she remained abroad. So I followed you on the next ship and met you at Sorrento, where I introduced myself as Count Ferralti--a name we had agreed I should assume before we parted in America.

"The rest of my story you know. My father was killed in an accident on his own railroad, and I received the news while we were prisoners of the brigand, whom I discovered to be my uncle, but who had no mercy upon me because of the relationship. To-night, on my return here, I found a letter from my father's attorney, forwarded from my bankers in Paris. Through my father's sudden death I have inherited all his wealth, as he had no time to alter his will. Therefore Mrs. Merrick's objection to me is now removed, and Louise has never cared whether I had a penny or not."

He halted, as if not knowing what more to say, and the little group of listeners remained quiet because it seemed that no remark from them was necessary. Young Weldon, however, was ill at ease, and after hitching nervously in his chair he addressed Uncle John in these words:

"Sir, you are the young lady's guardian for the present, as she is in your charge. I therefore ask your consent to our formal engagement."

"Not any," said Uncle John, decidedly. "I'll sanction no engagement of any children on this trip. You are wrong in supposing I am Louise's guardian--I'm just her chum and uncle. It's like cradle-snatching to want to marry a girl of sixteen, and you ought to be ashamed of yourself, for you can't be much more than twenty-one yourself. While Louise is in my care I won't have any entanglements of any sort, so you'll have to wait till you get home and settle the business with her mother."

"Very wise and proper, sir," said Mr. Watson, nodding gravely.

Louise's cheeks were flaming.

"Do you intend to drive Arthur away, Uncle?" she asked.

"Why should I, my dear? except that you've both taken me for a blind old idiot and tried to deceive me. Let the boy stay with us, if he wants to, but he'll have to cut out all love-making and double-dealing from this time on--or I'll take you home in double-quick time."

The young man seemed to resent the indictment.

"The deception seemed necessary at the time, sir," he said, "and you must not forget the old adage that 'all's fair in love and war.' But I beg that you will forgive us both and overlook our fault, if fault it was. Hereafter it is our desire to be perfectly frank with you in all things."

That was a good way to disarm Uncle John's anger, and the result was immediately apparent.

"Very good," said the old gentleman; "if you are proper and obedient children I've no objection to your being together. I rather like you, Arthur Weldon, and most of your failings are due to the foolishness of youth. But you've got to acquire dignity now, for you have suddenly become a man of consequence in the world. Don't think you've got to marry every girl that attracts you by her pretty face. This devotion to Louise may be 'puppy-love,' after all, and--"

"Oh, Uncle!" came a chorus of protest.

"What, you rascals! are you encouraging this desperate fol-de-rol?"

"You are too severe, Uncle John," said Patsy, smiling. "The trouble with you is that you've never been in love yourself."

"Never been in love!" He beamed upon the three girls with devotion written all over his round, jolly face.

"Then you're jealous," said Kenneth. "Give the poor kids a fair show, Uncle John."

"All right, I will. Arthur, my lad, join our happy family as one of my kidlets, and love us all--but no one in particular. Eh? Until we get home again, you know. We've started out to have the time of our lives, and we're getting it in chunks--eh, girls?"

"We certainly are, Uncle John!" Another chorus.

"Well, what do you say, Arthur Weldon?"

"Perhaps you are right, sir," answered the young man. "And, anyway, I am deeply grateful for your kindness. I fear I must return home in a couple of weeks, to look after business matters; but while I remain with you I shall try to conduct myself as you wish."

"That sounds proper. Is it satisfactory to you, Louise?"

"Yes, Uncle."

"Then we've settled Cupid--for a time, anyway. And now, my dears, I think we have all had enough of Taormina. Where shall we go next?"

CHAPTER XXVII
TATO IS ADOPTED

They canvassed the subject of their future travels with considerable earnestness. Uncle John was bent upon getting to Rome and Venice, and from there to Paris, and the nieces were willing to go anywhere he preferred, as they were sure to enjoy every day of their trip in the old world. But Mr. Watson urged them strongly to visit Syracuse, since they were not likely to return to Sicily again and the most famous of all the ancient historic capitals was only a few hours' journey from Taormina. So it was finally decided to pass a week in Syracuse before returning to the continent, and preparations were at once begun for their departure.

Kenneth pleaded for one more day in which to finish his picture of Etna, and this was allowed him. Uncle John nevertheless confessed to being uneasy as long as they remained on the scene of his recent exciting experiences. Mr. Watson advised them all not to stray far from the hotel, as there was no certainty that Il Duca would not make another attempt to entrap them, or at least to be revenged for their escape from his clutches.

On the afternoon of the next day, however, they were startled by a call from the Duke in person. He was dressed in his usual faded velvet costume and came to them leading by the hand a beautiful little girl.

The nieces gazed at the child in astonishment.

Tato wore a gray cloth gown, ill-fitting and of coarse material; but no costume could destroy the fairy-like perfection of her form or the daintiness of her exquisite features. With downcast eyes and a troubled expression she stood modestly before them until Patsy caught her rapturously in her arms and covered her face with kisses.

"You lovely, lovely thing!" she cried. "I'm so glad to see you again, Tato darling!"

The Duke's stern features softened. He sighed heavily and accepted Uncle John's polite invitation to be seated.

The little party of Americans was fairly astounded by this unexpected visit. Kenneth regretted that he had left his revolver upstairs, but the others remembered that the brigand would not dare to molest them in the security of the hotel grounds, and were more curious than afraid.

Il Duca's hand was wrapped in a bandage, but the damaged finger did not seem to affect him seriously. Beth could not take her eyes off this dreadful evidence of her late conflict, and stared at it as if the bandage fascinated her.

"Signore," said the Duke, addressing Uncle John especially, "I owe to you my apologies and my excuses for the annoyance I have caused to you and your friends. I have the explanation, if you will so kindly permit me."

"Fire away, Duke," was the response.

"Signore, I unfortunately come of a race of brigands. For centuries my family has been lawless and it was natural that by education I, too, should become a brigand. In my youth my father was killed in an affray and my mother took his place, seizing many prisoners and exacting from them ransom. My mother you have seen, and you know of her sudden madness and of her death. She was always mad, I think, and by nature a fiend. She urged my elder brother to wicked crimes, and when he rebelled she herself cast him, in a fit of anger, into the pit. I became duke in his place, and did my mother's bidding because I feared to oppose her. But for years I have longed to abandon the life and have done with crime.

"With me our race ends, for I have no sons. But my one child, whom you know as Tato, I love dearly. My greatest wish is to see her happy. The last few days have changed the fortunes of us both. The Duchessa is gone, and at last I am the master of my own fate. As for Tato, she has been charmed by the young American signorini, and longs to be like them. So we come to ask that you forgive the wrong we did you, and that you will now allow us to be your friends."

Uncle John was amazed.

"You have decided to reform, Duke?" he asked.

"Yes, signore. Not alone for Tato's sake, but because I loathe the life of brigandage. See; here is my thought. At once I will disband my men and send them away. My household effects I will sell, and then abandon the valley forever. Tato and I have some money, enough to live in quiet in some other land, where we shall be unknown."

"A very good idea, Duke."

"But from my respect for you, Signer Merreek, and from my daughter's love for your nieces--the brave and beautiful signorini--I shall dare to ask from you a favor. But already I am aware that we do not deserve it."

"What is it, sir?"

"That you take my Tato to keep for a few weeks, until I can send away my men and arrange my affairs here. It would be unpleasant for the child here, and with you she will be so happy. I would like the sweet signorini to buy nice dresses, like those they themselves wear, for my little girl, and to teach her the good manners she could not gain as the brigand's daughter. Tato has the money to pay for everything but the kindness, if you will let her stay in your society until I can claim her. I am aware that I ask too much; but the Signorina Patsy has said to my child that they would always be friends, whatever might happen, and as I know you to be generous I have dared to come to you with this request. I only ask your friendship for my Tato, who is innocent. For myself, after I have become a good man, then perhaps you will forgive me, too."

Uncle John looked thoughtful; the old lawyer was grave and listened silently. Patsy, her arms still around the shrinking form of the child, looked pleadingly at her uncle. Beth's eyes were moist and Louise smiled encouragingly.

"Well, my dears? The Duke is certainly not entitled to our friendship, as he truly says; but I have nothing against little Tato. What do you advise?"

"Let us keep her, and dress her like the beautiful doll she is, and love her!" cried Patsy.

"She shall be our adopted cousin," said Louise.

"Tato is good stuff!" declared Kenneth.

"Well, Beth?"

"It seems to me, Uncle," said the girl, seriously, "that if the Duke really wishes to reform, we should give him a helping hand. The little girl has led a bad life only because her father forced her to lure his victims and then procure the money for their ransoms; but I am sure her nature is sweet and pure, and she is so young that she will soon forget the evil things she has learned. So I vote with my cousins. Let us adopt Tato, and care for her until her father can introduce her into a new and more proper life."

"Well argued, Beth," said Uncle John, approvingly. "I couldn't have put the case better myself. What do you say, Silas Watson?"

"That you are all quite right," answered the old lawyer. "And the best part of the whole thing, to me, is the fact that this nest of brigands will be wiped out of existence, and Taormina be hereafter as safe for tourists as old Elmhurst itself. I wish I could say as much for the rest of Sicily."

Uncle John extended his hand to the Duke, who took it gratefully, although with a shamefaced expression that was perhaps natural under the circumstances.

"Look up, dear," said Patsy to the girl, softly; "look up and kiss me. You've been adopted, Tato! Are you glad?"

CHAPTER XXVIII
DREAMS AND DRESS-MAKING

Tato was now one of the family. They left Taormina the next day, and Frascatti drove all the girls in his victoria to the station.

"You must come again, signorini," said he, looking regretful at their departure. "Next year the fountain of the ice cream soda will be in operation, like those you have in Chicago, which is America. Our culture increases with our civilization. It is even hinted that Il Duca is to abandon our island forever. He has been interesting to us, but not popular, and you will not miss him when you come again to find he is not here. If this time he has caused you an inconvenience, I am sorry. It is regrettable, but,--"

"But it is so!" said Patsy, laughing.

Tato was again transformed. Patricia, who was the smallest of the three nieces, though not especially slim, had quickly altered one of her own pretty white gowns to fit the child, and as she was deft with her needle and the others had enthusiastically assisted her, Tato now looked more like a fairy than ever.

It was really wonderful what a suitable dress could do for the tiny Sicilian maid. She had lost her free and boyish manner and become shy and retiring with strangers, although when in the society of the three nieces she was as sweet and frank as ever. She wore her new gown gracefully, too, as if well accustomed to feminine attire all her life. The only thing now needed, as Patsy said, was time in which to grow her hair, which had always been cut short, in boyish fashion.

They were a merry party when they boarded the train for Syracuse, and Uncle John arranged with the guard to secure two adjoining compartments all to themselves, that they might have plenty of room.

"Where did you put the money, Uncle John?" Beth whispered, when at last they were whirling along and skirting the base of Mt. Etna toward the Catania side.

"I've hidden it in my trunk," he replied, in the same confidential tone. "There is no bank in this neighborhood to receive it, so I decided to carry it with us."

"But will it be safe in the trunk?" she enquired.

"Of course, my dear. Who would think of looking there for fifty thousand dollars? And no one knows we happen to have so much money with us."

"What did the Count--I mean, Mr. Weldon--do with his ransom?"

"Carries it in his satchel, so he can keep it with him and have an eye on it. It's a great mistake, Beth, to do such a thing as that. It'll make him uneasy every minute, and he won't dare to let a facchino handle his grip. But in my case, on the other hand, I know it's somewhere in the baggage car, so I don't have to worry."

The journey was a delightful one. The road skirted the coast through the oldest and most picturesque part of Sicily, and it amazed them to observe that however far they travelled Etna was always apparently next door, and within reaching distance.

At Aci Castello they were pointed out the seven Isles of the Cyclops, which the blind Polyphemus once hurled after the crafty Ulysses. Then they came to Catania, which is the second largest city in Sicily, but has little of historic interest. Here they were really at the nearest point to the mighty volcano, but did not realize it because it always seemed to be near them. Eighteen miles farther they passed Leontinoi, which in ancient days dared to rival Siracusa itself, and an hour later the train skirted the bay and Capo Santa Panagia and slowly came to a halt in that city which for centuries dominated all the known world and was more powerful and magnificent in its prime than Athens itself--Syracuse.

The day had become cloudy and gray and the wind whistled around them with a chill sweep as they left their coach at the station and waited for Kenneth to find carriages. Afterward they had a mile to drive to their hotel; for instead of stopping in the modern town Uncle John had telegraphed for rooms at the Villa Politi, which is located in the ancient Achradina, at the edge of the Latomia de Cappuccini. By the time they arrived there they were blue with cold, and were glad to seek the warm rooms prepared for them and pass the remainder of the afternoon unpacking and "getting settled."

"I'm afraid," said Patsy, dolefully, "that we shall miss the bright sunshine and warmth of Taormina, Tato."

"Oh, it is not always warm there, nor is it always cold here," replied the child. "Indeed, signorina, I have heard that the climate of Siracusa is very delightful."

"It doesn't look it," returned Patsy; "but it may improve."

The interior of the hotel was comfortable, though, however bleak the weather might be outside. A good dinner put them all in a better humor and they passed the evening watching the strangers assembled in the parlors and wondering where they had come from and who they were.

"That money," whispered Uncle John to Beth, as he kissed her good night, "is still as safe as can be. I've lost the key to my trunk, and now I can't even get at it myself."

"Lost it!" she exclaimed.

"Yes; but that won't matter. It's the big trunk that holds the things I don't often use, and if I can't unlock it no one else can, that's certain. So I shall rest easy until I need something out of it, and then I'll get a locksmith to pick the lock."

"But I wish you hadn't lost the key," said the girl, thoughtfully.

"Strikes me it's good luck. Pleasant dreams, my dear. I can fancy Arthur Weldon lying awake all night with his dreadful thirty thousand tucked under his pillow. It's a great mistake to carry so much money with you, Beth, for you're sure to worry about it."

The next morning when they came down to breakfast they were all amazed at the gorgeous sunshine and the genial temperature that had followed the dreary afternoon of their arrival. Syracuse was transformed, and from every window of the hotel the brilliant glow of countless flowers invited one to wander in the gardens, which are surpassed by few if any in the known world.

The Villa Politi stood so near the edge of a monstrous quarry that it seemed as if it might topple into the abyss at any moment. Our friends were on historic ground, indeed, for these quarries--or latomia, as they are called--supplied all the stone of which the five cities of ancient Syracuse were built--cities which in our age have nearly, if not quite, passed out of existence. The walls of the quarry are a hundred feet in depth, and at the bottom are now acres upon acres of the most delightful gardens, whose luxuriance is attributable to the fact that they are shielded from the winds while the sun reaches them nearly all the day. There are gardens on the level above, and beautiful ones, too; but these in the deep latomia are the most fascinating.

The girls could scarcely wait to finish breakfast before rushing out to descend the flights of iron steps that lead to the bottom of the vast excavation. And presently they were standing on the ground below and looking up at the vine covered cliffs that shut out all of the upper world.

It was peaceful here, and soothing to tired nerves. Through blooming shrubbery and along quiet paths they might wander for hours, and at every step find something new to marvel at and to delight the senses.

Here were ancient tombs cut from the solid rock--one of them that of an American midshipman who died in Syracuse and selected this impressive and lovely vault for his burial place. And there stood the famous statue of Archimedes, who used in life to wander in this very latomia.

"Once," said Mr. Watson, musingly, "there were seven thousand Athenian prisoners confined in this very place, and allowed to perish through starvation and disease. The citizens of Syracuse--even the fine ladies and the little children--used to stand on the heights above and mock at the victims of their king's cruelty."

"Couldn't they climb out?" asked Patsy, shuddering at the thought that some of the poor prisoners might have died on the very spot her feet now trod.

"No, dear. And it is said the guards constantly patrolled the edge to slay any who might venture to make the attempt."

"Wasn't it dreadful!" she exclaimed. "But I'm glad they have made a flower garden of it now. Somehow, it reminds me of a cemetery."

But there were other interesting sights to be seen at Syracuse, and they laid out a systematic programme of the places they would visit each morning while they remained there. The afternoons were supposed to be reserved for rest, but the girls were so eager to supply Tato with a fitting wardrobe that they at once began to devote the afternoons to shopping and dress-making.

The child had placed in Uncle John's keeping a liberally supplied purse, which the Duke wished to be applied to the purchase of whatever his daughter might need or desire.

"He wants me to dress as you do," said Tato, simply; "and because you will know what is fitting my station and will be required in my future life, he has burdened you with my society. It was selfish in my father, was it not? But but--I wanted so much to be with you--because you are good to me!"

"And we're mighty glad to have you with us," answered Patsy. "It's no end of fun getting a girl a whole new outfit, from top to toe; and, aside from that, we already love you as if you were our little sister."

Beth and Louise equally endorsed this statement; and indeed the child was so sweet and pretty and so grateful for the least kindness bestowed upon her that it was a pleasure to assist and counsel her.

Tato looked even smaller in girls' clothing than in boys', and she improved so rapidly in her manners by constantly watching the nieces that it was hard to imagine she had until now been all unused to polite society. Already they began to dread the day when her father would come to claim her, and the girls and Uncle John had conceived a clever plan to induce the Duke to let his daughter travel with them on the continent and then go for a brief visit to them in America.

"By that time," declared Louise, "Tato's education will be accomplished, and she will be as refined and ladylike as any girl of her age we know. Blood will tell, they say, and the monk who taught her must have been an intelligent and careful man."

"She knows more of history and languages than all the rest of us put together," added Beth.

"And, having adopted her, we mustn't do the thing by halves," concluded Patsy; "so our darling little brigandess must tease her papa to let her stay with us as long as possible."

Tato smiled and blushed with pleasure. It was very delightful to know she had such enthusiastic friends. But she was afraid the Duke would not like to spare her for so long a time as a visit to America would require.

"You leave him to me," said Uncle John. "I'll argue the case clearly and logically, and after that he will have to cave in gracefully."

Meantime the dainty gowns and pretty costumes were one by one finished and sent to the hotel, and the girls ransacked the rather inadequate shops of Syracuse for the smartest things in lingerie that could be procured. As they were determined to "try everything on" and see how their protégé looked in her finery, Tato was now obliged to dress for dinner and on every other possible occasion, and she not only astonished her friends by her loveliness but drew the eye of every stranger as surely as the magnet attracts the needle.

Even in Sicily, where the Greek type of beauty to-day exists more perfectly than in Helene, there were few to compare with Tato, and it was only natural that the Americans should be very proud of her.

Kenneth was sketching a bit of the quarry and the old monastery beyond it, with the blue sea glimmering in the distance. Sometimes he would join the others in their morning trips to the catacombs, the cathedrals or the museum; but the afternoons he devoted to his picture, and the others came to the gardens with him and sat themselves down to sew or read beside his easel.

Arthur Weldon was behaving very well indeed; and although a good deal of the credit belonged to Louise, who managed him with rare diplomatic ability, Uncle John grew to like the young man better each day, and had no fault whatever to find with him.

He was still rather silent and reserved; but that seemed a part of his nature, inherited doubtless from his father, and when he chose to talk his conversation was interesting and agreeable.

Kenneth claimed that Arthur had a bad habit of "making goo-goo eyes" at Louise; but the young man's manner was always courteous and judicious when addressing her, and he managed to conceal his love with admirable discretion--at least when others were present.

Uncle John's private opinion, confided in secret to his friend Mr. Watson, was that Louise "really might do worse; that is, if they were both of the same mind when they grew up."

And so the days passed pleasantly away, and the time for their departure from Syracuse drew near.

On the last morning all of them--with the exception of Tato, who pleaded a headache--drove to the Latomia del Paradiso to see the celebrated "Ear of Dionysius"--that vast cavern through which the tyrant is said to have overheard every whisper uttered by the prisoners who were confined in that quarry. There is a little room at the top of the cliff, also built from the rock, where it is claimed Dionysius sat and played eavesdropper; and it is true that one in that place can hear the slightest sound uttered in the chamber below.

Afterward the amphitheatre and the ancient street of the tombs were paid a final visit, with a stop at San Giovanni, where St. Paul once preached. And at noon the tourists returned to the hotel hungry but enthusiastic, in time for the table-d'-hote luncheon.

CHAPTER XXIX
TATO WINS

"This is funny!" cried Patsy, appearing before Uncle John with a white and startled face. "I can't find Tato anywhere."

"And her new trunk is gone from her room, as well as her gowns and everything she owns," continued Beth's clear voice, over her cousin's shoulder.

Uncle John stared at them bewildered. Then an expression of anxiety crept over his kindly face.

"Are you sure?" he asked.

"There can't be a mistake, Uncle. She's just gone."

"None of you has offended, or annoyed the child, I suppose?"

"Oh, no, Uncle. She kissed us all very sweetly when we left her this morning."

"I can't understand it."

"Nor can we."

"Could her father have come for her, do you think?" suggested Mr. Merrick, after a moment's thought.

"I can't imagine her so ungrateful as to leave us without a word," said Patsy. "I know Tato well, Uncle, and the dear child would not hurt our feelings for the world. She loves us dearly."

"But she's a queer thing," added Louise, "and I don't trust her altogether. Sometimes I've surprised a look in her eyes that wasn't as innocent and demure as she would have us imagine her."

"Oh, Louise!"

"And there's another reason."

"What is it?"

"She reformed too suddenly."

Uncle John slapped his forehead a mighty blow as a suspicious and dreadful thought flashed across his mind. But next instant he drew a long breath and smiled again.

"It was lucky I lost that key to the trunk," he observed, still a little ashamed of his temporary lack of confidence in Tato. "It's been locked ever since we left Taormina, so the child couldn't be tempted by that."

"She wouldn't touch your money for the world!" said Patsy, indignantly. "Tato is no thief!"

"She comes of a race of thieves, though," Beth reminded her.

"I wonder if Arthur's money is still safe," remarked Louise, following the line of thought suggested.

As if with one accord they moved down the hall to the door of the young man's room.

"Are you in, Arthur?" asked Uncle John, knocking briskly.

"Yes, sir."

He opened his door at once, and saw with surprise the little group of anxious faces outside.

"Is your money safe?" asked Uncle John.

Weldon gave them a startled glance and then ran to his dresser and pulled open a drawer. After a moment's fumbling he turned with a smile.

"All safe, sir."

Uncle John and his nieces were visibly relieved.

"You see," continued Arthur, "I've invented a clever hiding-place, because the satchel could not be left alone and I didn't wish to lug it with me every step I took. So I placed the packages of bills inside the leg of a pair of trousers, and put them in a drawer with some other clothing at top and bottom. A dozen people might rummage in that drawer without suspecting the fact that money is hidden there. I've come to believe the place is as good as a bank; but you startled me for a minute, with your question. What's wrong?"

"Tato's gone."

"Gone!"

"Departed bag and baggage."

"But your fifty thousand, sir. Is it safe?"

"It has to be," answered Uncle John. "It is in a steel-bound, double-locked trunk, to which I've lost the key. No bank can beat that, my boy."

"Then why did the child run away?"

They could not answer that.

"It's a mystery," said Patsy, almost ready to weep. "But I'll bet it's that cruel, wicked father of hers. Perhaps he came while we were out and wouldn't wait a minute."

"What does the hall porter say?" asked Kenneth, who had joined the group in time to overhear the last speech and guess what had happened.

"Stupid!" cried Uncle John. "We never thought of the hall-porter. Come back to our sitting room, and we'll have him up in a jiffy."

The portiere answered his bell with alacrity. The Americans were liberal guests.

The young lady? Ah, she had driven away soon after they had themselves gone. A thin-faced, dark-eyed man had called for her and taken her away, placing her baggage on the box of the carriage. Yes, she had paid her bill and tipped the servants liberally.

"Just as I suspected!" cried Patsy. "That horrid duke has forced her to leave us. Perhaps he was jealous, and feared we would want to keep her always. Was she weeping and miserable, porter?"

"No, signorina. She laughed and was very merry. And--but I had forgotten! There is a letter which she left for the Signorina D'Oyle."

"Where?"

"In the office. I will bring it at once."

He ran away and quickly returned, placing a rather bulky parcel in the girl's hands.

"You read it, Uncle John," she said. "There can't be anything private in Tato's letter, and perhaps she has explained everything."

He put on his glasses and then took the missive and deliberately opened it. Tato wrote a fine, delicate hand, and although the English words were badly spelled she expressed herself quite well in the foreign tongue. With the spelling and lack of punctuation corrected, her letter was as follows:

"Dear, innocent, foolish Patsy: How astonished you will be to find I have vanished from your life forever; and what angry and indignant words you will hurl after poor Tato! But they will not reach me, because you will not know in which direction to send them, and I will not care whether you are angry or not.

"You have been good to me, Patsy, and I really love you--fully as much as I have fear of that shrewd and pretty cousin of yours, whose cold eyes have made me tremble more than once. But tell Beth I forgive her, because she is the only clever one of the lot of you. Louise thinks she is clever, but her actions remind me of the juggler who explained his tricks before he did them, so that the audience would know how skillful he was."

"But oh, Patsy, what simpletons you all are! And because you have been too stupid to guess the truth I must bother to write it all down. For it would spoil much of my satisfaction and enjoyment if you did not know how completely I have fooled you.

"You tricked us that day in the mountain glen, and for the first time an Alcanta brigand lost his prisoners and his ransom money through being outwitted. But did you think that was the end? If so you failed to appreciate us.

"Look you, my dear, we could have done without the money, for our family has been robbing and accumulating for ages, with little need to expend much from year to year. It is all in the Bank of Italy, too, and drawing the interest, for my father is a wise man of business. That four hundred thousand lira was to have been our last ransom, and after we had fairly earned it you tricked us and did not pay.

"So my father and I determined to get even with you, as much through revenge as cupidity. We were obliged to desert the valley at once, because we were getting so rich that the government officials became uneasy and warned us to go or be arrested. So we consulted together and decided upon our little plot, which was so simple that it has worked perfectly. We came to you with our sad story, and you thought we had reformed, and kindly adopted me as one of your party. It was so easy that I almost laughed in your foolish faces. But I didn't, for I can act. I played the child very nicely, I think, and you quite forgot I was a brigand's daughter, with the wild, free blood of many brave outlaws coursing in my veins. Ah, I am more proud of that than of my acting.

"Innocent as I seemed, I watched you all carefully, and knew from almost the first hour where the money had been put. I stole the key to Uncle John's trunk on the train, while we were going from Taormina to Syracuse; but I did not take the money from it because I had no better place to keep it, and the only danger was that he would force the lock some day. But Ferralti's money--I call him Ferralti because it is a prettier name than Weldon--bothered me for a long time. At the first he would not let that little satchel out of his sight, and when he finally did he had removed the money to some other place. I searched his room many times, but could not find his hiding place until last night. While he was at dinner I discovered the bills in one of the drawers of his dresser.

"But for this difficulty I should have left your charming society before, as my father has been secretly waiting for me for three days. Having located Ferralti's money I waited until this morning and when you had all left me I signalled to my father from my window and prepared to disappear. It took but a few minutes to get the money from Uncle John's trunk and Arthur's trouser-leg. Much obliged for it, I'm sure. Then I packed up all my pretty dresses in my new trunk--for part of our plot was to use your good taste in fitting me out properly--and now I am writing this loving epistle before I leave.

"We shall go to Paris or Vienna or Cairo or London--guess which! We shall have other names--very beautiful ones--and be rich and dignified and respected. When I grow older I think I shall marry a prince and become a princess; but that will not interest you much, for you will not know that the great princess is your own little Tato.

"Tell Uncle John I have left the key to his trunk on the mantel, behind the picture of the madonna. I stuffed papers into Arthur's trouser leg to deceive him if he came back before I had a chance to escape. But I hoped you would discover nothing until you read this letter, for I wanted to surprise you. Have I? Then I am content. You tricked me once; but I have tricked you at the last, and the final triumph is mine.

"In spite of all, Patsy dear, I love you; for you are sweet and good, and although I would not be like you for the world I can appreciate your excellent qualities. Remember this when your anger is gone. I won't be able to visit you in America, but I shall always think of you in a more kindly way than I fear you will think of the Sicilian tomboy, TATO."

CHAPTER XXX
A WAY TO FORGET

The faces of the group, as Uncle John finished reading, were worth studying. Arthur Weldon was white with anger, and his eyes blazed. Silas Watson stared blankly at his old friend, wondering if it was because he was growing old that he had been so easily hoodwinked by this saucy child. Beth was biting her lip to keep back the tears of humiliation that longed to trickle down her cheeks. Louise frowned because she remembered the hard things Tato had said of her. Patsy was softly crying at the loss of her friend.

Then Kenneth laughed, and the sound sent a nervous shiver through the group.

"Tato's a brick!" announced the boy, audaciously. "Can't you see, you stupids, that the thing is a good joke on us all? Or are you too thin skinned to laugh at your own expense?"

"Oh, we can laugh," responded Uncle John, gravely. "But if Tato's a brick it's because she is hard and insensible. The loss of the money doesn't hurt me, but to think the wicked little lass made me love her when she didn't deserve it is the hardest blow I have ever received."

That made Patsy sob outright, while Louise ejaculated, with scorn: "The little wretch!"

"It serves us right for having confidence in a child reared to crime and murder from the cradle," said Arthur, rather savagely. "I don't know how much money I am worth, but I'd gladly spend another thirty thousand to bring this wretched creature to justice."

"Money won't do it," declared the lawyer, shaking his head regretfully. "The rascals are too clever to be caught in Europe. It would be different at home."

"Well, the best thing to do is to grin and bear it, and forget the unpleasant incident as soon as possible," said Uncle John. "I feel as if I'd had my pocket picked by my best friend, but it isn't nearly as disgraceful as being obliged to assist the thief by paying ransom money. The loss amounts to nothing to either of us, and such treachery, thank goodness, is rare in the world. We can't afford to let the thing make us unhappy, my friends; so cheer up, all of you, and don't dwell upon it any more than you can help."

They left Syracuse a rather solemn group, in spite of this wise advice, and journeyed back to Naples and thence to Rome. There was much to see here, and they saw it so energetically that when they boarded the train for Florence they were all fagged out and could remember nothing clearly except the Coliseum and the Baths of Carracalla.

Florence was just now a bower of roses and very beautiful. But Kenneth lugged them to the galleries day after day until Uncle John declared he hated to look an "old master" in the face.

"After all, they're only daubs," he declared. "Any ten-year-old boy in America can paint better pictures."

"Don't let anyone hear you say that, dear," cautioned Patsy. "They'd think you don't know good art."

"But I do," he protested. "If any of those pictures by old masters was used in a street-car 'ad' at home it would be money wasted, for no one would look at them. The people wouldn't stand for it a minute."

"They are wonderful for the age in which they were painted," said Kenneth, soberly. "You must remember that we have had centuries in which to improve our art, since then."

"Oh, I've a proper respect for old age, I hope," replied Uncle John; "but to fall down and worship a thing because it's gray-haired and out-of-date isn't just my style. All of these 'Oh!'s' and 'Ahs!' over the old masters are rank humbug, and I'm ashamed of the people that don't know better."

And now Arthur Weldon was obliged to bid good-bye to Louise and her friends and take a train directly to Paris to catch the steamer for home. His attorney advised him that business demanded his immediate presence, and he was obliged to return, however reluctantly.

Kenneth and Mr. Watson also left the party at Florence, as the boy artist wished to remain there for a time to study the pictures that Uncle John so bitterly denounced. The others went on to Venice, which naturally proved to the nieces one of the most delightful places they had yet seen. Mr. Merrick loved it because he could ride in a gondola and rest his stubby legs, which had become weary with tramping through galleries and cathedrals. These last monuments, by the way, had grown to become a sort of nightmare to the little gentleman. The girls were enthusiastic over cathedrals, and allowed none to escape a visit. For a time Uncle John had borne up bravely, but the day of rebellion was soon coming.

"No cathedrals in Venice, I hope?" he had said on their arrival.

"Oh, yes, dear; the loveliest one in the world! St. Mark's is here, you know."

"But no St. Paul's or St. Peter's?"

"No, Uncle. There's the Saluta, and the--"

"Never mind. We'll do that first one, and then quit. What they build so many churches for I can't imagine. Nobody goes to 'em but tourists, that I can see."

He developed a streak of extravagance in Venice, and purchased Venetian lace and Venetian glassware to such an extent that the nieces had to assure him they were all supplied with enough to last them and their friends for all time to come. Major Doyle had asked for a meerschaum pipe and a Florentine leather pocket book; so Uncle John made a collection of thirty-seven pipes of all shapes and sizes, and bought so many pocketbooks that Patsy declared her father could use a different one every day in the month.

"But they're handy things to have," said her uncle, "and we may not get to Europe again in a hurry."

This was his excuse for purchasing many things, and it was only by reminding him of the duty he would have to pay in New York that the girls could induce him to desist.

This customs tax worried the old gentleman at times. Before this trip he had always believed in a protective tariff, but now he referred to the United States customs as a species of brigandage worse than that of Il Duca himself.

They stopped at Milan to visit the great cathedral, and then raced through Switzerland and made a dash from Luzerne to Paris.

"Thank heaven," said Uncle John, "there are no cathedrals in gay Paree, at any rate."

"Oh, yes there are," they assured him. "We must see Notre Dame, anyway; and there are a dozen other famous cathedrals."

Here is where Uncle John balked.

"See here, my dears," he announced, "Not a cathedral will I visit from this time on! You can take a guide and go by yourselves if you feel you can't let any get away from you. Go and find another of Mike Angelo's last work;

every church has got one. For my part, I've always been religiously inclined, but I've been to church enough lately to last me the rest of my natural life, and I've fully determined not to darken the doors of another cathedral again. They're like circuses, anyhow; when you've seen one, you've seen 'em all."

No argument would induce him to abandon this position; so the girls accepted his proposal and visited their beloved cathedrals in charge of a guide, whose well of information was practically inexhaustible if not remarkable for its clarity.

The opera suited Uncle John better, and he freely revelled in the shops, purchasing the most useless and preposterous things in spite of that growing bugbear of the customs duties.

But finally this joyous holiday came to an end, as all good things will, and they sailed from Cherbourg for New York.

Uncle John had six extra trunks, Patsy carried a French poodle that was as much trouble as an infant in arms, and Louise engineered several hat-boxes that could not be packed at the last minute. But the girls embarked gay and rosy-cheeked and animated, and in spite of all the excitement and pleasure that had attended their trip, not one of the party was really sorry when the return voyage began.

CHAPTER XXXI
SAFE HOME

"To me," said Uncle John, as he stood on the deck and pointed proudly to the statue of Liberty in New York harbor, "that is the prettiest sight I've seen since I left home."

"Prettier than the old masters, Uncle?" asked Patsy, mischievously.

"Yes, or the cathedrals!" he retorted.

When they reached the dock there was the Major waiting to receive Patsy in a new checked suit with a big flower in his button-hole and a broad smile on his jolly face.

And there was Mrs. Merrick, too, with Arthur Weldon beside her, which proved to Louise that he had succeeded in making his peace with her mother. Also there were the stern-featured custom-house officials in their uniforms, and the sight of them sent the cold chills flying down Uncle John's spine.

There was no one present to receive Beth, but her uncle tucked her arm underneath his own with a proud gesture and kept her close beside him. For the girl had quite won his loving old heart on this trip, and she seemed to him more mature and far sweeter than when they had left home.

But the greetings and the "brigandage" were soon over, and in good time they were all assembled in the Doyle flat, where the joyous Major had prepared an elaborate dinner to celebrate the return of the wanderers.

"We've a million pipes and pocket-books for you, daddy," whispered Patsy, hugging him for the twentieth time; "and I've got a thousand things to tell you about our adventures in strange lands."

"Save 'em till we're alone," said the Major; "they're too good to waste on a crowd."

Mr. Merrick was placed at the head of the table to make a speech. It was brief and to the point.

"I promised these young ladies to give them time of their lives," he said, "Did I do it, girls?"

And in a lively chorus they answered:

"You did, Uncle John!"